the Hand of Buddha

STORIES

the Hand of Buddha

LINDA WATANBE McFERRIN

Coffee House Press

COFFEE HOUSE PRESS is an independent nonprofit literary publisher supported in part by a grant provided by the Minnesota State Arts Board, through an appropriation by the Minnesota State Legislature, and in part by a grant from the National Endowment for the Arts. Significant support has also been provided by the Bush Foundation; Elmer L. & Eleanor J. Andersen Foundation; General Mills Foundation; Honeywell Foundation; James R. Thorpe Foundation; Lila Wallace Reader's Digest Fund; Pentair, Inc.; McKnight Foundation; Patrick and Aimee Butler Family Foundation; The St. Paul Companies Foundation, Inc.; the law firm of Schwegman, Lundberg, Woessner & Kluth, P.A.; Star Tribune Foundation; the Target Foundation; West Group Foundation; and many individual donors. To you and our many readers across the country, we send our thanks for your continuing support.

COFFEE HOUSE PRESS books are available to the trade through our primary distributor, Consortium Book Sales & Distribution, 1045 Westgate Drive, Saint Paul, MN 55114. For personal orders, catalogs, or other information, write to: Coffee House Press, 27 North Fourth Street, Suite 400, Minneapolis, MN 55401.

LIBRARY OF CONGRESS CATALOGING-IN-PUBLICATION INFORMATION
McFerrin, Linda Watanabe, 1953–
    The hand of Buddha : stories / by Linda Watanabe McFerrin
    p. cm.
    ISBN 1-56689-104-3 (alk. paper)
    1. Women—United States—Fiction. I. Title
PS3573.A7987 H36 2000
813'.54—DC21   00-043099

10 9 8 7 6 5 4 3 2 1
FIRST EDITION / FIRST PRINTING

PRINTED IN CANADA

Contents

ACKNOWLEDGEMENTS

So many people inspired the stories in this collection. So many people encouraged me.

I'd be remiss if I didn't thank Josephine Smedley first—for being a pal, a right hand, and an advisor. I also want to thank Toni, Michele, the three Jacquelines, Mary Brent, Suzanne, Kris, both Susans, Colleen, Deanna, Erika, Sandi and Sandy, Marianne, Mary Ann, Genie, Amelia, Rena, Sita, Ann, Leigh Ann, Debbie, Terri, Kelley, Michelle, Laura, Lory, Lisa, Barbara, Jessica, Ruth, Nancy, Eriko, Margaret, Faith, Jenny, Seraphina, Maria, Cloteal, Gail, my ex-colleagues at LS&CO., my writing buddies, all the students in my writers' workshops, John, Paul, Charles, Bill, Perry, Rick, and of course, my dear little Braveheart; for their love, inspiration, and friendship.

A special thank you to Joan and Bill Flint, Francine Ringold, Ruth Hardman, Manly Johnson, Elaine Petrocelli, Alice Acheson, Victoria Shoemaker, John Flinn, Donald George, the Wild Writing Women, Allan Kornblum and the good people at Coffee House Press, and my best editor, Lowry McFerrin, for their support and professional direction. I wouldn't have written this without you!

for the Wild Writing Women

Foreword

Some of my stories have exotic settings. This is because, for me, place has tremendous texture and interest. As a travel writer, I'm obsessed with romantic places and faraway lands, but often, when I'm looking for a story, I can't get any further than my own backyard—my Vietnamese neighbor, Mrs. Vu, and her struggle for identity; my sister with her dual interests in romance and spirituality; a friend whose illness has opened a door to art, or a colleague who is trying to put her life back together after the death of her husband. I believe that whatever is compelling in literature is pulled from life, often daily life, and the ongoing struggles that propel us from one day to the next.

As a travel writer, I wander the globe. Many of my friends, also lovers of travel, roam the planet as well. My environment is a diverse one and the stories gathered here reflect and rejoice in that. I live, by preference, in a city of many cultures. Asian, Hispanic, African American, Caucasian—citizens of many ethnic backgrounds have come to settle, here, in Oakland. To step out of our doors is to step into adventure.

Most importantly, the stories and characters in this collection are inspired by the lives and personalities of women who are dear to me, women who I am lucky enough to know and love.

This collection is in celebration of their lives.

— Linda Watanabe McFerrin

Coyote Comes Calling

Sam, a.k.a. Samantha Iphigenia Darwin, d.b.a. Sam's Wampum Wigwam, Main Street, Sedona, Arizona, was having a coyote week. She hadn't realized this yet, but what she did know was this: certain things were going wrong.

It started when she dumped a bottle of the wrong color hair dye on her head. Her amber locks turned brassy blonde. Then she had a flat tire on the way back from Scottsdale where she'd gone to her doctor. Her visit, precipitated by the sudden hyperextension of her abdomen, ended in her gynecologist's assessment that Sam either had a large fibroid tumor or she was pregnant. They'd know for sure in a couple of days. At the time of this pronouncement, Sam's legs were spread, her feet up in the pink potholder-protected stirrups.

"I don't know, Sam," her doctor, Sally, observed, "I fear it's a fibroid tumor."

"What's that? Is it cancer?"

"Well, no. But, if it is a fibroid tumor, we'll have to remove it."

"Shit," Sam said, letting out a low whistle.

"On the other hand, you could be pregnant."

"What?" Sam asked, incredulous, fearing a pregnancy almost as much as a tumor. "What will I do with a baby? I'm not even married."

"You can still have a baby, Sam."

"That's not what I mean, Sally. It's just not in my reality. Besides, that would mean the baby is Daryl's."

"What's wrong with that?"

"Sally, we're talking *Daryl*. You know, Mr. Noncommitment. Fly Boy. Permanent Puer. It's like saying Peter Pan is the dad. It's that serious."

"It's not that bad, Sam. Anyway, we'll know in two days."

"We'll know in two days." That's what Sam was thinking about when a piece of shrapnel jumped up off the road and speared her sidewall. She heard the hissing first, like a snake. She rolled down the window and listened. The snake was following her. Naturally, she didn't have a jack, at least not one that worked. It was that kind of week. She had a spare tire, but she'd broken the jack months ago when she helped Cynthia, her best friend in the world, fix a flat in the Coffee Pot parking lot. She kept telling herself to replace it. She hadn't, and now she was "paying the price of procrastination," as her mother would have said.

Fortunately, she was close to Sedona and home when the tire started to hiss. It shouldn't have been hard to flag down some help. However, as luck would have it, her realization of the equipment shortfall corresponded with a certain unpleasant coincidence. At the exact moment that she realized that the jack

Linda Watanabe McFerrin

was not going to work, a certain primer-brown pickup appeared on the shaky horizon. It quivered toward her like a mirage. It was the worst thing that could have possibly happened. It was Daryl's truck.

"Your savior again," Daryl said with a wide grin as he swung his long legs out of the truck. Beau, his obedient hound, jumped out, too.

Just what she did *not* want to hear. But being in something of a bind, Sam let him change her tire. Sam hated herself for letting him do it, and she was sullen when she arrived at her store, Sam's Wampum Wigwam, Main Street, Sedona.

Erly, her helper, had already been in that morning and stacked the packages neatly on the counter. Sam was grateful for Erly. Erly was her only support. She was a tough little woman, originally from New York, and she was generous, dependable, and a darn hard worker.

You've got to see beyond the surface, Sam reminded herself, standing in the middle of the roomful of trading beads, prayer feathers, and amulets.

"Erly is a perfect example of squirrel energy," Sam thought, stringing totems.

Sam needed a little time with her thoughts. It had been a terrible morning. This baby. What in heaven's name was she going to do? An abortion, probably. Sam couldn't have a baby. She couldn't let an infant into her life. It was hard enough washing her own hair, feeding herself every day. Getting from one place to another was a perpetual challenge. She had trouble staying balanced and managing her own needs. How could she do it for two?

The shop door opened. This was a great surprise. It was March, and Sam's Wampum Wigwam survived mainly on mail order at this time of year. Noting that it was David, her pal, and the man she'd recently decided she'd most like to go to bed with, Sam immediately broke into a glossy cover-model smile. The thought of her swollen belly ragged at her.

"Hey, David," she said cheerfully, "I thought you were in Phoenix this week. What's going on?"

"Oh, I came back early," David said in his soft purr of a voice. David had the kind of voice that could coax eggs out of a rooster.

"Sam," David said, "I have a favor to ask."

"Sure," said Sam. "Anything. What'll it be?"

"Well," he said, suddenly shy (Sam found this endearing), "I wonder if I could get Cynthia's number from you. I'm thinking of asking her out."

Sam felt as though she'd been kicked by a mule in the solar plexus, right over that little tumor.

"Yeah, sure," she heard herself say quickly, hiding her surprise. "I'll give you her number."

She wrote down the number and handed it to him. She was amazed that her hands weren't shaking. She felt reasonable, even calm. She suspected she was in some kind of shock.

Sam saw herself standing on top of Apache Leap. Below her,

Cynthia and David were putting around on the green of the world's most obnoxiously situated golf course. It was built over an Indian burial ground. Sam hated that golf course. She, Sam, alias Wile E. Coyote, was rolling a boulder to the edge of the precipice. She was going to drop it on the spoony-eyed couple below. She imagined it squashing them both. Then a breeze came out of nowhere, ruffling her hair. It was the "Wind of Karma."

"That boulder," it said, "is going to bounce like a superball. It is going to hit the golf course lighter than angel food cake and bounce back on you with the force of a Peterbilt truck. Don't do it, Sam."

"Thanks, Sam," David was saying. He'd completed his morning mission, and already had one leg out the door. "By the way, I don't know what you've done with your hair, but it looks great."

"Tasteless goon," Sam thought, as he left. But she knew that if he asked her to go out, she'd say yes. Sam felt like she'd taken a ride in the spin cycle.

"What a rotten day," she thought miserably. "What else can go wrong?"

That's when she noticed the squashed package on the counter. It was from Bella, the Italian bead manufacturer. Her Venetian trading beads—she'd been waiting for them for months. She needed them to fill one of her store's largest orders. She had a very bad feeling about this. She opened the package. It was filled with glittering powder—sea blue, gold, bottle green—beads ground to dust. On the package wrapper was a note: "This package was damaged in transit. Please file a claim."

There are times when it all gets to be too much for you and you just have to close up shop. This was one of those times. Sam could feel a couple of big fat cow tears running down the sides of her nose.

"That does it," she said.

She turned out the lights and flipped over the sign on the door to read "closed."

Sam didn't want to see anyone. Not Cynthia, Daryl, Erly, or David. She wanted to be alone. She jumped into her car and headed for home. That's when she saw him, standing at the side of the road. The mangy, yellow-eyed dog; the trickster; the hound of the desert; her new pal—Wile E. Coyote. The coyote was standing there, mouth pulled back in a panting grin. Its big yellow eyes connected with hers—full of promise, full of mischief, full of sorrow—and suddenly it let out a quick little yelp. Actually, it was more like a greeting. That is when Sam realized that she was having a coyote week.

"Okay, little brother," she said to the animal. "I get it. Things are out of my control. Nothing I can do."

Sam understood totems. She knew that an armadillo at the side of the road meant that she wasn't watching her boundaries, that when mountain lions appeared it was time to take a leadership role. She knew that a lynx meant secrets, a fox camouflage, and she knew that the best posture to take during a coyote week was what she called "baby in a car crash." You had to go limp and unresisting. You had to relax or you'd really get hurt.

So Sam took the cosmic advice. She drove to the bakery and picked up a bag of warm chocolate chip cookies. Then she stopped by her house and picked up some thai stick to roll more than a couple of joints and headed for Cathedral Rock, a powerful feminine vortex on the high red rocks of Sedona, a place where the energy collects and swirls. She climbed until she felt as though she were sitting on top of the world. She could see the Coffee Pot restaurant, HO-scaled in the canyon. The long line of hoodoos, spires, and minarettes of sandstone that crawled along the horizon made her think of the skyline of an Eastern empire.

"Dr. Seuss," she thought. "It looks like a Dr. Seuss landscape."

Sam sat cross-legged on the ground. She could feel the earth humming up under her skirt. She meditated, smoked a joint, meditated some more, and ate all of the chocolate chip cookies. She was thinking of Daryl, of babies, of abortion.

"Everything is a risk," she thought. "None of us is ever really in control. Our authority is all an illusion."

She imagined a cute little cherub that looked just like her—the same amber hair, Daryl's blue eyes. "How could I possibly prefer a tumor to that?" she wondered. "I must be out of my mind." It was true that a baby might send her over the edge, but she was a capable woman. She ran her own business. Daryl or not, she could make it work.

The day slipped out from under her. Evening bore down. It grew dark and cold. Sam made an anthill of cornmeal in front of her. She threw a pinch of it over her shoulder: cornmeal offering. With a pocketknife, she ripped open one corner of her down vest: prayer feather offering. She lit the end of a smudge stick—a bundle of herbs tied together with string— and waved it around, letting the sage perfume the air. With the same match, she lit another one of the joints and took a long slow drag. The night snuggled in around her. The stars moved in a little bit closer.

"Daryl," she thought, "is not such a terrible guy." Too bad he was constantly taking her out where the water was high or the road too narrow. Careless Daryl generally found some way to expose the people around him to danger. But he did always seem to come through. "Your savior," he'd said. That was a laugh. He was more like her nemesis.

Sam took another drag from her joint, counting coup—the gains and the losses. The problems came tumbling in. The whispy vest down was lifting and drifting around her in a whirlpool of wind. It looked like snow flurries. She leaned back on her elbows and watched it. She watched the stars come sliding closer, between the down, like little souls settling on earth— like babies.

The hard red Sedona rock was digging into the small of her back. The night air was kissing her cheeks. She was happy and sad at the same time. How weird the world was. How beautiful. How full of problems. At some point, you just had to relax. You had to trust someone, even if it was only yourself. That's exactly what she was thinking when the tumor kicked her. She swore

Linda Watanabe McFerrin

that it did. She was shocked. It was a swift kick in her gut, that was certain. She even let out a moan. Somewhere in the cool desert night the coyotes heard her moan, and they answered. First one, then another, in a great chain of song until the night was filled with coyote music. Sam was almost moved to tears by the magic of it. Then the tumor kicked her again, and she let out a war whoop, a laugh, and a big coyote howl.

"Praise the Lord. Hell's bells," Sam shouted in a spontaneous evangelistic frenzy, embracing the possibilities. This coyote week could turn into a coyote life.

Meantime, all around her, the dogs were singing.

Los Mariachis del Muerto

(The Musicians of Death)

Isabella was contemplating the nature of Death and, incidentally, the meaning of Life. At nineteen, she was pretty and bright—not yet the radiant beauty that she would later become—her luminosity being of the kind that brought to mind the Virgin of Guadalupe, which perhaps accounted for her perennially unmarried status since Celestial auras have a way of discouraging ordinary suitors, although it could be argued that her single state had been brought about by the death of the infant and other significant events that took place in her nineteenth year.

The child was not Isabella's, nor did it belong to the Anglo couple, Señor and Señora Stetson, for whom she worked. The child that died had been in the care of Iñez Felicia Casa-Contide, another of the brown-skinned young women who worked in the Anglo households of Santa Fe and who made up the social community of well-employed Mexican girls that was Isabella's.

That Iñez was in no way responsible for the child's death, and could in no way be held culpable, was a miracle. Sometimes when people—Anglos, anyone—are in grief, they reach out with long fingers of blame to pull others into their misery. So it was a good thing that the baby had died during the night when Iñez was safely home and asleep in her tiny, twin bed in the small house on the outskirts of Santa Fe where she lived with her mother, three sisters, and two brothers. At one time the family had hoped that Iñez would be asked to move in with the Morrisons, the couple she worked for. Iñez had resisted. Her mother, sisters, and brothers thought she was crazy, but it turned out to be a very good thing that Iñez did not move in with the Morrisons. If she had accepted, she would have been there when the infant died, and the death would have surely been attributed to her negligence. The Anglo doctor's pronouncement was that the Morrison infant had died of seeds. That is what Iñez reported to the other maids when they gathered to hang their washing.

"Seeds?" Isabella asked.

"Yes, sí, seeds. The poor little creature choked in the night." Iñez crossed herself. "Such a precious hijo. He must have choked on the seeds."

"Oh, my goodness," Isabella exclaimed. "Did *you* feed the baby the seeds?"

"No, Isabella," reported Iñez. "And the family, they are so fine, they never even accused me."

"That's very strange. Muy extraña," said the other maids, knowing that if the children in their care were to choke to death on seeds they would certainly be found at fault.

Isabella thought this was extraordinary, too—not that the baby should die in this manner, but that Iñez had not been

Linda Watanabe McFerrin

blamed. She could not reconcile it with the way she knew things were between maids and their Anglo employers. So, at dinner as she served up the sopa for her Señor and Señora, she mentioned the death of the Morrison infant and the manner of the baby's death.

"The Doctor Minton," she reported, "he says that Iñez's baby died of seeds."

"Seeds?" Señora Stetson queried, her pale blue eyes fluttering as they did when she was confused.

"Yes, seeds," repeated Isabella. "You know, he choked. Suffocated. He must have eaten too many of them."

"Seeds?" the Señora repeated, considering the word. "Died of seeds? That's very strange." Her blue eyes fluttered for a while longer, then stopped and went very pale. They were looking inward, searching her mind. Isabella had noticed that the Señora did this when she was thinking very hard.

Isabella continued. "Such a tiny baby," she said sadly. "Of course, it was very foolish to feed him seeds." The Señor wore a worried expression. His eyes went from Isabella to Lauren, his wife.

"Seeds," Lauren, the Señora repeated, "Hmmm . . . seeds." Then, all at once, the light went on. The clouds parted; the Señora's eyes brightened; the blue rushed back into them.

"Oh, Isabella," she corrected. "I think you mean SIDS. Yes, that's what Doctor Minton must have said—SIDS. Sudden Infant Death Syndrome. Many infants die this way. No one knows why. They just seem to stop breathing. Yes, yes, the doctor must have said SIDS. Don't you think so, Rob?"

"Sounds logical," said the Señor, his brows unknitting, glad to see the confusion leaving the face of his wife. The Señor didn't like confusion. He would be upset if he felt that Isabella were generating a little pool of confusion in their otherwise organized world.

Isabella's coffee complexion flushed burgundy. She was embarrassed now about the "seeds." She knew that the Señor and Señora were right. An Anglo doctor would make an Anglo diagnosis.

Lauren placed her soup spoon precisely upon the china charger beneath her bowl. "Yes, yes," she said happily, glad to have cleared up the misunderstanding, "the doctor must have said SIDS."

"SIDS," Isabella repeated as she cleared the soup course, angry at herself for her foolish mistake. She was mad at the other maids too for their ignorance, but a part of her mind backed away from the pat explanation of the Señor and Señora Stetson. Sudden Infant Death Syndrome. That still didn't explain it. Why did the baby die?

Isabella knew better than to pursue the subject that evening. She served the fish course, then the salad. She finished this all with dessert, which the Señor ate with relish and the Señora declined. The latter part of the meal progressed without incident, and when it was finished, the Señor and Señora retired to

　　　　　　　　　　　　Linda Watanabe McFerrin

their separate corners to read. From the window of her pleasant garden cottage, Isabella could see the light on by the Señora's bedside. It glowed eerily in the upstairs window of the adobe-style home until late that evening when the shadow that was the Señor bent over the shadow that was the lamp and put it out.

The next day, Isabella informed the other maids about how mistaken they were.

"But what does that mean?" asked LaRosa, the oldest and fattest of them all. LaRosa was thirty-eight years old. She had raised two boys to manhood in the household she worked for and had single-handedly raised four children of her own at the same time. All six children loved LaRosa. She was more a mother to the two Anglo boys than their own. LaRosa had great authority. She would not accept an Anglo fact without examining it very, very closely.

"It means nothing," LaRosa declared, throwing all of her weight and authority against the rationale of the Stetsons, against the Anglo doctor. "The little boy suffocated," she summarized, "that we all know. But we still do not know the cause." LaRosa sounded extraordinarily wise and powerful when she spoke in this manner. She was almost a bruja. If she were in Mexico, she would have a house paid for by the village, and the people would bring her gifts.

"Iñez," she said, addressing the pretty young maid. "Iñez, I think you have the answer. Why don't you tell the others about the Smurfs?"

"The Smurfs?" Iñez repeated, hypnotically, eyes on LaRosa. "Oh, girlfriends, they are terrible!" Iñez was recollecting the little acid-blue creatures that had been scattered about the blessed baby's nursery. They were scrawny, pin-headed dolls with long noses and evil grins. They were very bad objects for sure. Very wicked.

"The baby, he liked them," she recalled sorrowfully, referring to the terrible Smurfs. "If I took them away, he cried. But they were jealous of the hijo," she reported. "They are dreadful and nasty, those Smurfs."

"Tell us how the infant died," LaRosa demanded.

"Yes, yes I will tell you," Iñez said softly. "The Smurfs—they suffocated him."

A group gasp escaped from the ample and lovely bosoms of all the maids. This they could believe. Iñez had, on occasion, shared stories with them of her battle over the Smurfs. She had suspected their evil intentions. She had tried to keep them out of the nursery, but the baby had fussed, his parents had become concerned, and the Smurfs had remained in the Morrison infant's bed.

"Have you mentioned this to the Señor and Señora Morrison?" Isabella asked warily.

"Oh, no," said Iñez. "I wouldn't do that. They get very angry when I say things like that. They are very upset now. I don't want them to get mad at me."

"Iñez is right, of course," LaRosa announced firmly. "It was the Smurfs that killed the baby. They sucked the life from his little chest."

"Yes, the Smurfs, the Smurfs," the other maids nodded. "They killed Iñez's charge."

That evening Señor Stetson was running. He ran every Thursday night, all along the Paseo de Peralta and up Artist Road, past Ten Thousand Waves, the spa on the hill. He ran ten miles every Thursday without fail. Isabella thought it was very strange that he ran so hard and so long. "Just like a horse," she thought to herself. "Why would a man do that?" Isabella made him a cold plate on those nights and set it aside for his dinner. If Señor Stetson had been in the house, she would not have mentioned the Smurfs. He wasn't, so when Lauren—Señora Stetson—sat down to her dinner at the long table, Isabella told her about the Smurfs and Iñez and LaRosa's conclusions about how they had smothered the baby.

"Yes, it was strange for them to think this," Isabella hedged, "but Iñez and LaRosa are certain that the evil deed was performed by those horrible blue creatures."

Mrs. Stetson's face registered a quick succession of emotions. First her blue eyes gave a small flicker of confusion; then they widened in disbelief; then her rose-colored mouth opened in a small oval of awareness; then, finally, her pleasant, small-featured face rearranged itself in a smile.

"Isabella," she said, brushing a stray wisp of ash-blonde hair from her forehead. "Isabella, don't you realize Smurfs are only toys? Toys cannot kill an infant."

Isabella looked down at her black slip-on shoes. Mrs. Stetson's feet, visible just under the table, looked neat in their perfectly groomed, beige suede boots.

"I didn't believe it anyway," Isabella insisted. "Iñez and LaRosa are too superstitious."

"Yes," said Lauren. "That's right, Isabella. Now," she asked lifting her napkin and placing it carefully upon her lap, "what have you made us for dinner?"

The next day, Mr. Stetson called Isabella into the library. "Isabella," he said, "you have me somewhat disturbed." Isabella knew what he was planning to say.

"This business about the baby that died—the seeds and the Smurfs—you realize, don't you, that this is all nonsense?"

Isabella nodded glumly. It had been a mistake to confide in the Señora.

"I hope," Mr. Stetson concluded, "that you are simply reporting what you have heard. You do not believe these things. Superstition is a very dangerous thing," he continued. "It comes of ignorance. It breeds misapprehension. I don't want to think that you support or display this behavior."

"Señor," Isabella mumbled, "you know I was just repeating what Iñez and LaRosa had told me."

"Then you know that this is just ignorance talking. Good, Isabella," the Señor said kindly, "I'm glad that we had this talk."

Linda Watanabe McFerrin

Isabella did not go back that Friday to the little Plaza de las Glorias laundromat where the maids gathered to hang and fold washing. The environment of the maids was once her whole world, but the baby's death had changed all of that. It was funny, she thought, how something seemingly unrelated to something else could cause such a great deal of change. Suddenly she no longer wanted to see Iñez and LaRosa and the other maids. Their large brown eyes and smooth faces reflected back an image of herself that embarrassed her. She did not want to see them and say, "It wasn't the Smurfs at all!" They would argue with her, of course. They were stubborn and insistent. Their world wouldn't change. But the Señor and Señora, Isabella sighed, all the Anglos—they were stubborn and insistent too. Much more stubborn in fact, than her own people. Still, theirs was a way that she hadn't yet tried. She must look into it further. She must give it a chance.

So, Isabella quite consciously turned her back on her old friends. She enrolled in the local community college. She signed up for math and history and science in a single semester. The Señor and Señora Stetson were amazed. They were also visibly pleased. Once again Señor Stetson called Isabella into his library. This time he said, "Isabella, my friend who teaches at the community college says you have signed up for his class. Is this true?"

"Yes," Isabella nodded, looking down at her feet. "Yes, I am going to history class with Señor Betterly, and I am taking math and science, too, Señor.

"Well, that's fantastic, Isabella," he boomed. "Why didn't you tell us?"

Isabella had learned her lesson; she had not confided in the Señora. But the teacher, Betterly, he had told the Señor. Anglos, she concluded, cannot keep secrets.

Señor Stetson was pacing the carpet in his excitement. He was running his hand through his hair.

"This is wonderful, Isabella," he said. "The future will open up for you. Opportunities will be yours. Of course, selfishly, I worry that it means that we'll lose you."

Isabella blanched when he said this. The last thing she wanted was to lose her job. "No, Señor," she started to say, but he stopped her.

"No matter," he continued, "that will come later. In the meantime, you will study. You will learn. I like to think that in some way I influenced this decision," he said soberly, stopping his pacing, turning to her and looking into her eyes with great meaning.

Isabella couldn't return his gaze, "Yes, Señor Stetson, you did," she mumbled. She was afraid that she might not have done the right thing. She looked down at the carpet with its thunderbird design. She saw a great big pool of confusion spreading out and filling the library.

The next day at dinner the strange magic started. The Señor and Señora Stetson presented Isabella with a very large check. A bonus, they said, to help with her education.

Isabella stared at it in disbelief. She couldn't believe her good fortune. She wanted to share this marvelous news, so in a cinnamon-and-orange-colored skirt, a fresh white blouse, and well-polished black shoes, she headed for the Plaza to see her old friends.

"Isabella, Isabella," they started to say, as she walked in the door, "we have missed you. Have you been ill?" But they noticed, almost immediately, the bright colors of her skirt, the starched crispness of her blouse, and the shine on her shoes, and they knew that there was more to it than this.

"Oh," gasped Iñez, "Isabella, you are in love."

Isabella looked out through the window. She didn't want to lie to her friends.

"No," said LaRosa, "Isabella isn't in love—love looks much softer than this."

"Isabella," she asked, her voice husky and rough so that it sounded like a man's, almost like the voice of Señor Stetson. "Isabella, what is this about?"

"School," Isabella managed to squeak, feeling like a traitor. She no longer wanted to share the news of her good fortune. Somehow her good fortune felt like a very bad thing. "I am going to go to school."

LaRosa arched one eyebrow, then the other. "Aha," she said with a dark smile. "Our ways are no longer enough."

Isabella shrugged her shoulders helplessly.

"You will see," said LaRosa in a deep and prophetic voice.

"You will see, Isabella, that the Anglo ways are also not enough. But," she added portentously, "I may have the answers you seek. Remember our revelation about the Smurfs, Isabella. Things are not always as they seem."

Isabella left feeling uncomfortable. She did not seek out LaRosa again.

All spring and summer Isabella took courses at the community college. She learned about theorems and constants. She learned about gravity, chaos, and centrifugal force. She learned about tyrants, western imperialism, and manifest destiny. Her brain sometimes felt as if it would explode with all of the things she learned. Other times it felt like a sieve or a colander, all the knowledge running out of it as fast as she put it in. But mostly she felt like an impostor, especially when Señor Stetson would quiz her about her studies. She would answer him, hearing herself saying the words, wondering what in the world she was talking about. But she would see Señor Stetson nodding with a grave expression on his face. And she would hear him say, "Yes, yes, that is right, Isabella. You are certainly right about that."

Señora Stetson also seemed pleased with her progress. "You know, Isabella," she said, "there is a logic to the way you do everything these days. Like the way you serve dinner and the way you put the clothes in the drawers—long-sleeved shirts on the bottom, short-sleeved shirts on the top."

Isabella used to put all the Señora's favorite clothes on the

Linda Watanabe McFerrin

top so that they would be easy to get to. With the new arrangement, Señora Stetson began to wear clothes that she used to wear rarely, largely because they didn't look good on her. These days the Señora didn't look as handsome and perfectly dressed as she used to, but she was happy. Only Isabella felt that things were really not right.

Isabella knew that all the information that she was feeding her brain was not quite falling into place. She had piles of facts, but they didn't really explain anything. The more she learned, the more understanding eluded her. Her quest for answers brought only more questions. Her logic led her down some interesting paths, but in the end it led nowhere. She seemed, always, to be going back in by the same door through which she came out. But she had to admit, she was doing quite well in her studies. She was in the top two percent of all her classes, and her teachers were urging her to transfer to a four-year college. Her classmates asked her opinion on everything, and the Anglo boys were in awe of her brilliance. This was really the beginning of this tendency of Isabella's to inspire awe in the opposite sex, a trait that persisted for most of her life. So, in spite of a fundamental disconnect between Isabella's mind and the knowledge that filled it, everything about Isabella's shift in perspective seemed designed to propel her toward greater and greater success. Now three lights were on at night in the Stetson household—one in the library, one in Señora Stetson's bedroom, and one in the cottage behind the big house. Three lights. Three readers. Three trains of thought.

As for the other maids, Isabella rarely saw them anymore. Once or twice she ran into Iñez at the market or one of the others downtown, but the meetings were always somewhat awkward. They were embarrassed by the changes in Isabella, and she was embarrassed, too.

It was at just such a chance meeting, early in October, some weeks into her third semester in college, that Isabella ran into Iñez on the busy sidewalk in front of the Palace of the Governors. Iñez looked terrible. Her eyes were all puffy and red. She looked as if she'd been crying for days.

"Iñez, what's wrong?" Isabella asked, grabbing her friend's arms. Her love for Iñez rushed into her heart. Her friend's sadness almost overwhelmed her.

Iñez's face registered nothing but shock. "Oh, Isabella," she gasped, "you mean you don't know?"

"Don't know? Don't know what?" Isabella asked, genuinely surprised.

"LaRosa," Iñez blurted out with great force in her speech, "LaRosa is dead."

Isabella stood for a moment, dumbfounded by the news. LaRosa was dead. Impossible. She felt as if she were standing alone in the middle of a vast mesquite-and-cottonwood-dotted plain. It was just like the one near Santa Clara Pueblo where she'd gotten lost as a child. It was noon, very hot, and the vultures were circling overhead. She thought they were circling for her, but it turned out that they were circling for a cow with a big,

Linda Watanabe McFerrin

swollen stomach. It lay on its side, its legs like four clothespins sticking straight out. Isabella approached the cow cautiously. It was still alive, but the flies were already crawling all over its face. She brushed them away with a long branch, but they came back. The buzzards continued to circle. Isabella kept walking, trying to find her way back to her parents, but she succeeded only in putting more distance between them. When they finally found her, having mobilized the whole pueblo, everyone was unhappy. Isabella was not hugged and kissed. She was scolded.

Iñez's sweet round face appeared suddenly, looking concerned, from behind an imaginary cottonwood tree.

"Isabella," she asked, "Isabella, are you all right?"

"Sí," Isabella said quickly. "How? How did LaRosa die?"

"It was very strange, Isabella," Iñez replied in a whisper, as if worried that someone might overhear. "LaRosa had a small mole on her stomach, and it got larger and larger until it was the size of a hand—the size of a tarantula spider. And it looked like a spider, too—furry and dark and of a very strange shape. LaRosa showed it to us one day. She said the shadows were growing inside her. They were turning her inside out. The mole, it grew very fast, and the next thing we knew, LaRosa was dead. Of course, we never told Father Quito what LaRosa had said. He might not have given her the sacraments."

"It was good that you didn't tell Father Quito," Isabella nodded approvingly. Father Quito had not always agreed with LaRosa. An ongoing war, defined by a repetitive series of skir mishes during which the young women usually sided with LaRosa, marked their relationship. In spite of this, LaRosa's faith was never debated. She was very religious. But it irked Father Quito that she and the other young Mexican women were more drawn to the tales of the miraculous, the ceremony and pomp of the Catholic Church, than its rules and its dogma. LaRosa would want the last sacrament. It was good that she wasn't denied it.

"When did LaRosa die?" Isabella asked, trying to place this disaster in the sensible framework of time.

"Over a month ago," Iñez replied sheepishly. "I'm sorry we didn't tell you, Isabella, but we never saw you to tell you. We thought you were angry with us. We knew you were upset with LaRosa. LaRosa kept saying you would be back, but you didn't come back, so we figured you'd abandoned us for your school and your studies."

Isabella swallowed hard and nodded. She could see how they would all think that. Still, it distressed her to have missed LaRosa's funeral, to have never offered a prayer, and she was greatly disturbed by LaRosa's death. What had caused the sudden growth of the mole? How had it killed LaRosa?

She went to her books for the answers. She read about melanoma and cancer. She read about chemotherapy, radiation, and bone marrow transplant. She read about macrobiotic diets and peach pits and papaya enzymes. She didn't come up with one satisfactory answer—not one—and she found herself back where she'd started, back at the death of the Morrison infant

Linda Watanabe McFerrin

with the big dark blot of LaRosa's mole growing between her and her understanding.

Isabella decided to see Father Quito. She made an appointment and spoke with him face-to-face. It was hard to ask this man all her questions, to expose the confusion that pooled about her without the dark grillwork that protected her in the confessional. She sat stiffly on one of the leather-covered Spanish-style chairs in Father Quito's office. A two-foot statue of the Virgin of Guadalupe, hands outstretched, clad in blue and lit from below, looked down peacefully upon her from a small ledge built into the stucco wall. Isabella noted, with some surprise, how much she resembled this particular rendition of the Virgin of Guadalupe. Father Quito noticed, with a febrile little twinge of pleasure, exactly the same thing.

"Isabella," he said, "LaRosa has gone to a better place."

At this, the puddle of confusion around Isabella ceased its amoeba-like maturation. Her agitation instantly disappeared. Her face rearranged itself, becoming as impassive as the face of the plaster Virgin on the wall above her. What was Father Quito saying? What in the world did that mean? Nothing. He was telling her exactly nothing.

Father Quito could see that the pearl of wisdom that he had presented to Isabella as his answer, and that generally met with profound success when offered to the other members of his flock, was not having the desired effect. She had shut every window of her shimmering, silvery little soul and retreated to the depths of her own ruminations. Her brown eyes became as dark and guarded as the grillwork of the confessional.

"Isabella," he squeaked, trying again, desperately wanting to win her back, "remember, we are having service for the Feast of All Saints, the Día de los Muertos, in two weeks. Come to the service, spend the day in contemplation; make your peace with LaRosa then."

He knew, in his heart, that this would appeal to Isabella. The church would be filled with incense and the smoke of candles lit for the departed. Bright flowers would festoon the crosses in the little graveyard next to the church. There would be small sugar skulls stacked like bricks on every gravesite, and the ants would march merrily back and forth, giddy with sugar, in their long processionals over the mounds. "Heavenly Father," he prayed, "I know that I am playing right into their hands, but really what else can I do?"

"Beyond the grave," he whispered to himself. It was one more of LaRosa's skirmishes and, once again, she had won. The Virgin of Guadalupe seemed to smile down on him, too, her face luminous, her carnelian mouth gently mocking.

But it worked.

"Yes, yes, Father Quito," Isabella was saying. "You are right. That would be a good time to offer my prayers." It still wasn't the answer, but maybe she would find one in the sanctuary of the church on that very significant day. Yes. Yes, the Día de los Muertos—surely if she were ever to find the answers she sought, that would be the time and the way.

Linda Watanabe McFerrin

"Thank you, Father Quito," Isabella said, executing a spontaneous curtsy.

"Of course, my child," Father Quito said humbly, taking her small hand, quite proud of himself for doing the expedient thing. It had worked after all. He felt guiltless and strangely elated.

All Saints' Eve arrived at the appointed time, to be celebrated by each culture in its own way. There were cats, witches, and ghosts in some of the neighborhood windows. The Señora Stetson wouldn't dream of decorating her home in that manner, but she had arranged several large and beautiful gourds in hefty Indian baskets on either side of the entrance, and she had three big bowls of candy ready for Isabella to hand out to the children that invariably came to the door. Greeting Halloween trick-or-treaters was Isabella's job, so she went to church early that day and stayed until almost twilight.

She walked home in the dusky late afternoon, still dizzy from the incense, the candle smoke, the murmur of prayers, her knees red and bruised from repetitive genuflections. She had no time to reflect upon the effect of the prayer or to sort out the tumble of emotions and images that rolled through her heart and mind.

The first little children were already on the walk when she arrived, and she had to hurry to intercept them at the door.

"Trick or treat," said a tiny red devil, barely breathing behind his mask. "Trick or treat," said a midget gypsy and an oddly outfitted teenage boy with eyeliner around his eyes and two pillow sacks, both filled with candy. Isabella kept dropping the candy bars into their pumpkin buckets and their bags, and they kept coming—witches, goblins, dinosaurs, Smurfs (Yes, Smurfs. At least she thought one of them was a Smurf.), genies, dancing girls, gangsters, ghouls, cowboys, vaqueros, skeletons—lots of skeletons—and fairies. Isabella was exhausted by the time they quit coming, and the hour was late. It was almost eleven o'clock. The Señor and Señora had already retired to their separate corners to read.

When she stepped out into the garden, Isabella realized why the children had kept coming. It was a perfectly beautiful night out. In the Stetsons' backyard, the adobe wall that surrounded the garden screened out all but the loftiest breezes. These faintly stirred the trellised roses, threading the cool night air with the most delicate strands of fragrance. Under the moonlight, on the dark carpet of grass, the bell-shaped flowers of the wild onions sparkled like miniature galaxies of stars, and the smell of grass and wild onion rose up and dissolved like the smoke of small votive candles. Tiptoeing the flagstones, Isabella made her way to her cottage. She glanced back at the house. Every light was off except one in Señor Stetson's library and one in Señora Stetson's bedroom. Isabella turned her light on and prepared for bed. She slipped out of her black shoes, out of her dress, and into her white cotton nightgown. She folded back the floral coverlet of her bed—she wouldn't need the extra blanket—and turned out the light. She lay there in the dark and the silence for a moment. Then she turned the light on again, quickly, stepped to the window and opened it, letting its two halves swing outward toward the garden. She could still see the lights on. Señor and Señora Stetson were still reading. Seeing the lights reminded Isabella of her studies, so she went to the closet, took her big history book out of her bag and opened it to the section about the Overland Trail. What did she expect to find on those pages? Reasons for things? Order? The stagecoach and mail carriers did not hold her interest, so she found herself nodding off now and again, the point of her chin hitting her sternum and jarring her back into a muddled consciousness.

It was on one of those quick jerks back out of slumber that she heard the music. It was soft at first, as she fought her way back from her dreams. Then it grew louder, and soon she was wide awake and amazed by the caterwaul in the garden just outside her window. "The Señor and Señora will be very upset," she decided as she stuck her head out of the window to see where the noise was coming from.

Isabella almost couldn't believe her eyes. Arranged in a half-circle facing her window, in the middle of the grassy lawn, were six mariachis. Four had guitars, one had a xylophone, and one had a fiddle. All wore enormous sombreros, but the strangest thing of all was that these mariachis were skeletons.

"Shoo, go away," hissed Isabella, like an angry goose. These children in skeleton costumes were playing a noisy trick on the household. The Señor would be furious. But when she looked at the bright square that was the library window, she noticed no flicker of movement. In shock, Isabella looked at the mariachis. It was impossible that the Señor hadn't heard them. They were wailing away, strumming their guitars and howling in high nasal singsongs. She noticed that each one was wearing some kind of weapon. One wore a machete at his waist. One wore a pair of big pistols. One had a couple of ammunition belts over each shoulder, criss-crossing over his chest, and another had a lariat tied at his waist. One had a rifle, and one had a bullwhip strapped to his back.

Isabella could see right through them, too. She could see through the narrow slats of their ribs, through the long skinny ladders of vertebrae to the house where the two windows glowed like the lopsided eyes of a jack-o-lantern. The skeletons strummed away, clicking their teeth together like castanets, raising their voices even louder. They advanced toward the window, rattling and clanking with every step. Oh, what a din they created! The crook of each finger made a sharp snap like a twig. The tilt of each head made a sound like a string of firecrackers exploding. And the music—the keys of the xylophone, which the player would lift and carry whenever the others took even two steps, were made of bones arranged on a metal frame rotten with rust. The strings of the guitars, which were certainly made of catgut, produced a sound like twelve cats being pulled by their tails. The maracas threatened like rattlesnakes, and the violin yelped and squealed as if it were being tortured. And the song—no sirocco had ever whined its way through a ghost town with a more wretched moan, no Mexican poet ever more plaintively lamented lost love.

Linda Watanabe McFerrin

All in all, between their art and their antics, the mariachis produced a dissonant but delightfully lively music, and Isabella felt it entering through her ears, massaging her mind, and rocking her insides with laughter. And as she listened, she realized they were singing about LaRosa.

"Where, oh where did my beloved LaRosa go-o-o-o," one of the skeletons moaned.

The others responded in a chorus of howls. "Oh-o-o," they yelped.

"Oh, I don't think man or woman will ever know-o-o-ow," the morbid mariachi continued. And, again, the others howled back their agreement.

"Do I care what the priest and the doctor said-ed-ed?"

"Noooooo," the skeleton chorus moaned.

"All I can say is my darling is dead dead dead dead."

They had wailed themselves into a frenzy, and every bone in their bodies was by this time clicking away in a fabulous percussive finale. Isabella found herself humming and repeating the last lines of the song to herself. "All I can say is my darling is dead dead dead dead." It seemed so conclusive, so certain. "LaRosa," she thought, "I think this is your answer."

Isabella felt her whole body relax. The skeletons nodded— clatter, snap, clatter; swept their sombreros from their heads—rattle, creak, pop; and bowed. Isabella applauded softly. The light went off in the library, and a few moments later the one in the bedroom went out.

Rubber Time

"How about Guam? I think that could be erotic. Why don't you write about Guam?"

"He's got to be kidding," Tamara thought. "What could possibly be erotic about Guam?" Besides, she'd never been there.

"Okay," she said, "sure, I'll give it a try." She would give him Malaysia and disguise it as Guam. They must be similar. Tamara wondered, "Were there rubber trees in Guam?"

The girl walked along the embankment, not three feet from the jeep. Kenneth could almost reach out an arm and touch her. They were moving forward in inches—traffic jam up the road and people on foot. Minutes stretched into hours. "Rubber time," he thought, "Guam."

Last night he had run the Lion City Hash with Norm and his harriers—twelve miles through jungle and cemetery. Then they got drunk. Rubber time in his head. Rubber time in his body. He was tired and hungover. Coconuts, split, by the side of the road, rotting fruit, heat, a fetid smell, like graves turned over—he was feeling nauseous. But, he was acutely aware of the girl, her thin arms a smooth chestnut-brown. She was soon out of reach, striding past him, still independent like the other young girls; not like the infant-carrying Indian women with the red smudges between their brows, the layers of dress, flower garlands, dragged down by the weight of breasts and bellies, the heavy lacquer upon their toenails. So many people walking along; it was like a river running past on the road—Chinese, Indian, Japanese, Malay. A break in the traffic—he caught up with the girl. Moving slowly, with purpose, so close he could smell her—musky, a mixture of sandalwood, jasmine, curry spices. Kenneth started to salivate.

"Old letch," he thought.

On the distant horizon—billowing green forest, red earth, clouds pregnant with rain. Closer in—lines of rubber trees, frail as wraiths or ghosts, long forked trunks leaning into one another, like women with their hands to their foreheads, bleeding the milky latex from their newly opened veins. In Kota Tinggi, the girls had been swathed in scarves and veils. Anonymous. The young ones in blue and white; the older ones in bright fuchsias pinks, oranges—female colors like jungle blossoms, also scarved and draped, also anonymous. Their smiles broke out and faded quickly. These people blossomed early; wilted swiftly. No shelter beneath the anemic rubber trees.

Again, the girl had outdistanced him. Kenneth Cormack McGinnis watched her skirt past the other pedestrians, her narrow hips hypnotic under blue and white silk. Her movement slid, like a penknife, down through his gut, up through his penis. His foot slipped on the gas pedal. The jeep lurched forward. The driver in front of him stuck his head out the window and let out a string of abuse.

Linda Watanabe McFerrin

Tamara pulled her story off the printer, stacked the pages, and tucked it away in the top desk drawer. "Enough of this nonsense," she scolded herself. "Don't go getting 'literary,' girl. This is not what the client is asking for. Toughen up. Get back to the task at hand. Remember, it's literal and clitoral."

She started writing again:

Caprice threw a muscular brown thigh over Donald. She wore nothing beneath the sarong skirt. He felt himself pinned, his belly damp under the soft, wet kiss of her genitals.

Her breasts, plump and juicy as a pair of jackfruit, dangled tantalizingly over his face. He closed his eyes and moaned.

"I think you better come with me, Donald," she said. "I get you there much faster."

She filled his mouth with a dark nipple the size of a thumb.

Donald's discipline flew out the window. The fine ladder of his ascetic aspirations crumbled. His consciousness did a nosedive from the painstakingly attained purple turret of his seventh chakra down to the pleasurable pig-style of his first.

"Damn you, Caprice," he managed to choke out as he grabbed two big handfuls of her firm, sticky flesh, pulled her into position, and plunged once more into pussy nirvana.

Story number twelve—done. Tamara licked the manila envelope closed and popped it into the mail. The envelope was marked, "To be opened by addressee only." This was her gig. She was making money. There was client demand. She worked on referral. It occurred to her that it was, in some ways, an unsavory enterprise. Someone, a man—as yet, she had no female clientele—would call her on a friend's recommendation. He would call her business number. He would say, "Hello, my name is so-and-so. Mark (or Mitchell or Daniel or someone) told me about you. I'd like a story about the New Hebrides. Let's say I was stranded there . . ."

"How many pages?" Tamara would interrupt. "Ten? Twenty?"

"Oh, I think ten would do."

"It's hard to develop a plot in ten pages."

"Who says it needs a plot?"

"Very well. Any special circumstances? Requests?"

"Yes. Very animal sex."

"Who?"

"I don't know. Whoever is in the story with me. Isn't that up to you?"

"Do they need to be women?"

"Absolutely, what do you take me for?"

"Don't get excited, I'm just trying to get all the specs."

"That's all I want to say."

"Very well, then. I'll use my imagination."

"Yes, please. How much will this be?"

Tamara would think for a moment. New Hebrides, huh? She'd have to do research. "Ten pages. No plot. That'll be $500."

"Five hundred dollars" the voice would come back, somewhat startled. "That's more than I expected."

"I'm good," she would say.

"Yes, I've heard," the man would respond. "All right, $500."

"When I get your check, I'll send the story."

"But what if I don't like it?"

"Don't worry, you will," Tamara would say. "I have only satisfied customers."

"Yes, well, thank you," the man would say.

"Any time," Tamara would answer. "Any time."

Then Tamara would bat out an erotic story, no holds barred, all stops out. And when the check came in the mail, she'd drop the story into its plain brown wrapper and post it. Sometimes she'd get calls—lascivious calls. But, hell, she could handle that, too. She'd say, "Look, there's plenty more where that came from."

After she mailed off the Guam story, Tamara headed for Soizic, her favorite lunch spot. She met Jerry there. Jerry looked awful.

"Jerry," she said, "you look awful."

"I hate my fucking job," Jerry announced, launching, without preamble, into his usual routine. "I'm a dull, boring hack writing copy for crap-ass products and sucking up to a bunch of corporate dildos."

"You have a foul mouth, Jerry." Tamara pulled a look of disgust.

"I can't help it. I'm frustrated. It's my only release," he whined.

Tamara shrugged. She'd heard it before. She'd heard it for ten years—all the time she'd known Jerry, her companion in print, or absence thereof.

"Change your name to Anon," she advised.

"Tamara, do you think for one minute that I actually sign the shit that I write? Hey, Anonymous is my corporate title. And what about you, kid?" he added archly. "How's your little enterprise?"

"My Communications Consulting Business is doing just fine," Tamara replied loftily. "I'll need to start farming out work soon."

"Don't forget your friends, baby," Jerry said sourly. "The people you meet heading north are the same ones you meet heading south."

"Your style's too bony, Jerry. You haven't got enough juice."

"Juice. I'll show you juice," he bragged, starting to get up.

"You know," Tamara said, quickly changing the subject and relieved when Jerry fell back into his chair, "island adventures are the latest trend. Believe it or not, so are dude ranches. Those are really a hoot. De Sade in dee saddle."

"Tamara," Jerry teased, "you know I love it when you talk like that."

"Jerry, please," she pleaded, "don't encourage me. I'm disturbed and dangerously close to the edge. I keep thinking about Tourette's Syndrome—brooding over it. I'm afraid I'll be suddenly overwhelmed with a desire to spit out scatological invectives. It scares me. I'm starting to see penises everywhere. I feel like I'm on the verge of hysteria. The line between reality and fantasy seems to be disappearing. I'm . . ."

Jerry held up a cautioning hand, "Wait just a minute," he interrupted. "Now, don't go getting weird on me, Tam."

"You mean you don' t want to listen to me? I thought you were different," she said with disgust.

Jerry pushed his chair from the table and stood, making a big scene about looking at his watch.

"Whoops, sorry Tamara, gotta go. It's 11:15. Time to get back to work."

"What is this?" Tamara snapped. "The new fifteen-minute lunch?"

"Yeah, well, you know, Tamara, that place is a salt mine. Same time tomorrow?"

"All right, fine." Her feelings always were guaranteed to clear a room. "All right, eleven o'clock tomorrow." She watched Jerry all but run from the restaurant.

"Shit," she thought as she left the table, silently scorekeeping (one point for Tourette's). "No one wants to listen to me. All these big-egoed men want to hear about is themselves. Just a bunch of large, pulsating dicks looking for a place to lodge." Tamara smiled as a man brushed by her, imagined him as that. He saw her smile and smiled back.

"Not with you, at you," she thought.

She knew why he was smiling. She saw her own wide shoulders and great pecs, the cut of her jacket accentuating these attributes to perfection. She saw her thick, ash-blonde hair, full lips, and freckles under big hazel eyes. She was really an eyeful, a "dish."

When she got back to her flat, the phone was ringing. She

noticed the queue of messages—six on the counter. She did not want to answer the phone. She let the machine do its job. She was moving toward some crisis, and she didn't like it. She opened the bottom drawer of the file cabinet and pulled out a bottle of Jack Daniels and a Dixie cup. "Good old Dad," she thought warmly, "my bad habits."

The liquor stung its way down her esophagus, fell with a plop into her stomach, and began to glow there—a small pool of incandescence. "Ah, much better," she thought, calmer, the furies once more at bay. The warmth began to spread to her limbs. "Ambrosia," she sighed, pouring another Dixie cup's worth of nectar, and opened the top desk drawer. Tamara put her boots up on the desk and flipped through her story.

He was so funny, this man, and he had a nice smell like tea leaves and bay rum. Nikki hoped he would not go away. He'd offered her a ride to town, and she had accepted. But then they had inched along and laughed about how futile it was to try to get anywhere, quickly, by car. He pointed out how the monkeys were mocking them, noisily, as they dangled from trailers of vine that draped the scarred trunks of the rubber trees. One of them, busily farming the thatch of fronds that roofed the forest, plucked some of the fat yellow and green fruit from its nest in the branches of the coconut palms and threw it at them. A slow-moving target is easy to hit. It glanced off the windshield. "You are not entirely safe," the man had forewarned.

Linda Watanabe McFerrin

She knew that she wasn't safe. Especially now. They sat on the crusty lip of a stream clogged with scabrous logs, having carelessly abandoned the jeep at the roadside. They had both taken off their shoes and thrust bare feet into the lizard-green water. Nearby, the earth was a snaggle of palm stumps. A few kinky-furred, caramel-colored sheep grazed on what little they could find. The man was laughing and talking, pointing out this tree and that. She was thoughtfully studying his legs. He was wearing shorts and must wear them most of the time because his legs were a light mahogany brown under their vapor of golden hair. They were strong-looking legs, lean and hard-muscled, and his thighs, which were revealed to the joint by the very short shorts, were taut and rod-like, even at rest. His feet, by contrast, now submerged in the murky shallows, were white, almost blue. Like pale fish, they stirred under the water's algae-furred surface—closeted creatures of darkness.

"Look." The man pointed high overhead. "Those clouds look like temples." Above them, gray peaks of cloud, thick with monsoons, rose in great columns, in layer upon layer of wall.

Nikki nodded and threw back her head, her dark brows raised, her mouth open in an expression of innocent awe. Her legs, too, were exposed to the thigh. She had drawn up her skirt and tucked it beneath her so that her legs hung, bare, over the banquette of hard ground. Kenneth wanted to slide a hand up the smooth sweep of her thigh. The hot humid afternoon seemed to gather itself about him. He was perspiring slightly. He wanted to lean toward her, explore her mouth with his tongue, the pliant chamber between her legs with his hands. "One quick move, and you'll scare her," he thought with an experienced hunter's patience. "Take it easy, old man."

Tamara's reverie was interrupted again by the insistent ring of the phone. The message machine clicked on.

"Hello, is this Tamara? This is Ted Wilson, again. I am a friend of Jason Newby. Jason recommended . . ."

"That guy again," Tamara thought. She remembered his voice from an earlier message. "What the hell, a client," she reminded herself. She picked up the phone. "Hi, this is Tamara."

"Oh, hello there." The caller sounded surprised and a little nervous. "My name's Theodore. Ted. You know Jason Newby?"

Yes, Jason Newby—adventure erotica: cliff-hangers, escape scenarios. "Ah, yes, Jason," she said.

"Right. Well, I liked Jason's story."

"Voyeur? Homosexual?" Tamara queried tartly.

Laughter. "Well, no. I hope that isn't a problem. Let me explain. I'd like a story, a story for my magazine."

"Do you have something in mind?"

"Well, no, not really. Just something along the lines of what you wrote for Jason."

"So, no other specs?" Tamara was feeling distrustful and cranky. A magazine. Yeah, right. She was tired of these men and their games. "Well," she said airily. "I happen to have something already written—a piece set in Guam. Since you aren't particularly selective, I could send that story to you."

"Sure. Sure, that would be great."

"How much does your 'magazine' pay?"

"How much are you used to getting?"

"Fifty dollars a page. This story's seventeen pages."

"Well, that's a little high."

"Nothing less."

"All right, fine. $850. I need it right away."

"No problem," Tamara said. "Here's how it works. You send me a check, I'll send you the story."

"Okay, Tamara," he said. "Where do I send the check?"

"What a waste," Tamara thought as she hung up the phone. She picked up her story, the one she'd just finished, and thumbed through it again. Well, if someone was willing to pay money for a story she cared about, she was certainly ready to sell her heart down the river. It was sad to her, though, to think of this particular story thrust into the top drawer of somebody's bedside table or the locked drawer at work. It was a damn good story. It deserved a better fate. What a waste.

So Tamara was more than a little surprised when a check arrived, via messenger, from Ted Wilson, Editor, *Compendium: A Journal for Men.*

"Heck," Tamara whispered, exhaling rapidly. "That guy was for real."

She posted the story with real pleasure. Posted it and waited for the response. She thought about Ted, Ted Editor as she'd mentally baptized him, opening the envelope. She could see him now, sitting at his desk reading it, turning the pages slowly, becoming aroused, getting up to close the door . . .

Ted Editor didn't call. A week passed by, then another. No word. Tamara couldn't stand it. Was he going to use the story? Did he like it? Had he even read it? Surely if he'd read it, he would have telephoned. She decided she'd wait one more day. She checked her answering machine almost every hour, scrolling through messages. Nothing from him. Frustration was not a feeling she liked. She rang him up at his office.

"Hi, yes, Tamara, I got the story. I read it. It was a little, well, unexpected. I can't use it in the magazine."

"Uhhh," Tamara said, stunned. "You editors sure know how to reject. So," she said, regaining her aplomb, "do you want your money back?"

"Nooooo." Tentative. "I liked it. I liked it a lot."

"Do you want another one?"

"Well, I'm afraid I've just about blown my personal story budget," he said with a laugh.

"Well, okay." Tamara said weakly. "Sorry you couldn't use it." She hung up feeling depressed.

It's funny the way people insinuate themselves into your life. All Tamara could think about for the next couple of months was Ted Editor's voice. He'd been so nice to her on the phone. A big fat rejection wrapped up in a kind male voice. It made her feel sick. What did she have? A couple of "likes." "I liked it. I liked it a lot." It bothered her. He didn't love it. He wasn't even going to use it.

But he "liked" it, and he had paid her $850 out of his own pocket.

So what was the big deal? Other guys paid. Yes, but they had gotten just what they'd asked for. This time she had sent a little piece of herself, and it was not what this man had expected, but he had liked it anyway. "Damn," she thought. "I should never have sent that to him." Now she was feeling some kind of personal connection, some weird obligation.

She tried to explain this to Jerry, her best and possibly only true friend.

"Ah, yes," Jerry said sagely, his fleshy lips pursed. "The Other, the Fugitive Other. The Reader for Whom We All Write."

"Oh, shut up, Jerry," Tamara snapped. "You're always making fun of me."

"You know, Tamara," Jerry had said, suddenly serious. "I don't think you really appreciate me." And there was something in his voice that made Tamara start to cry. And as the big teardrops rolled down her cheeks and her nose became swollen and red, Jerry ordered a couple of Bombay martinis and told stories about the "Gestapo Princess," his favorite corporate client, over the tears and the gin.

Jerry's narrative only made Tamara feel worse. Had she become like him, she wondered, a chronic depressive? The thought made her more miserable still. She struggled through the next couple of days, falling back into bad habits, drinking and hungover, until she could no longer stand it. Tamara yanked up the phone and quickly punched in the number of Ted Editor as she had done a number of times, hanging up when his answering machine responded. This time, to her surprise, she got the real guy. A mellow, male voice answered.

"Ted, here."

"Uh, hello," she said, off-balance. "This is Tamara." She didn't like the way her voice sounded—girlish, mousey-shy.

"Tamara? Tamara!" The recognition was nearly instantaneous. "Well, hi, Tamara." He seemed pleasantly surprised.

"Look, Ted," Tamara said, "I'm going to send you another story. I'm going to try again, okay?"

"Tamara," he said, "Don't. Really, it's all right."

"No," she insisted, "it's not. No charge. I *want* to do it."

"Tamara," he asked suddenly, "are you okay?"

"Yeah," she said, "yeah, I'm okay. I think I'm okay. No, hell, I'm not okay. And it has something to do with you and that stupid story and your rejection of it."

"Tamara, I liked your story. I told you I liked it."

"Yeah," she said, "well, what exactly did you like about it?"

"Well, let's see, I liked the girl, Nikki. I liked the way you pulled me deliciously along from page to page. And I liked it when you wrote," he paused, *"His mouth moved expertly up her thigh, his tongue hard, leaving a trail of warmth. Her legs parted reflexively. Hands on her hips, he pressed her up toward him. She felt as if she were ascending, rising up to the towers of clouds, high overhead."*

Tamara felt herself melt. She had to sit down. "You remember what I wrote?" she asked, incredulous.

Linda Watanabe McFerrin

"I have the story right here on my desk," he answered. "Listen, Tamara," he added, "I'm a little worried about you. Why don't you come over. Meet me here at the office. We can have a drink together. Talk."

"I usually don't meet my clients," Tamara said warily.

"Well, this is different, isn't it? Come over. I have some time. You have the address."

"I can't."

"Why?"

"Why? Because I'm coming unglued!"

"All the more reason," he said quietly.

"All right," Tamara agreed. "All right. I want to meet you."

"A cold shower, that's what I need," Tamara thought as she hung up the phone. The water was bracing. Things still felt surreal. Maybe it was the alcohol. She drank two cups of coffee. She was still feeling shaky. "Rubber time," she thought. Rubber time in her head. Rubber time in her body.

Ted Editor's office was in downtown Oakland. It was on the eighth floor. The elevator climbed slowly. Tamara was nervous. Her palms were sweating. By the time she got to the door, she was hoping he'd left for some reason, that he wouldn't be there. She knocked. No one answered. She cracked open the door. It was a gray and white office, the furniture—black leather and chrome. She noticed the slick magazines neatly fanned on the tables. Obscure literary journals, in volumes, lined the shelves. Tamara stepped inside. The office was dark, deserted. On the wall behind the front desk was a large lithograph of a voluptuous blue woman. Bisected on the vertical axis, half her body was naked. The other half was further exposed, her internal organs, blue-tinted, visible in perfect detail. Beneath her, a band of Times Classic type read, *Compendium: A Journal for Men.*

"Well, this is it," Tamara thought as she drew in her breath.

A thin slice of light cut the floor behind the right side of the lithographed wall. Tamara tiptoed toward it. It came from a door just around the corner. Tamara rapped on the door and opened it.

"Excuse me, Ted?"

She caught him completely off guard. "Oh, Tamara," he said, surprised, looking up from his work. "I didn't hear you come in."

He rose and walked around the desk toward her, nearly tripping on one of several piles of manuscripts stacked on the floor in front of an adjacent credenza. Not a graceful maneuver. He lurched forward, nearly falling against her.

"Sorry," he said, smiling.

"No problem," Tamara responded, looking up at him. He was tall, over six-three. She realized that he did not look the way she'd expected, only because she had not pictured him in her mind's eye. He was a little on the heavy side. He had dark brown hair, shot with gray, and wore wire-rimmed spectacles. He extended a hand and guided her, through a minefield of books and submissions, to a chair. Then he sat at his desk. He swept aside the manuscripts stacked in front of him. He leaned forward. The light hit

Linda Watanabe McFerrin

his glasses and bounced off, leaving an impenetrable glare. All Tamara could see were the mirror-like surfaces of the lenses. She couldn't see his eyes. He seemed distant, remote, a passionless intellectual. She had a cottony taste in her mouth, the way she always felt on small boats at sea.

Ted didn't say a word. He stared at her for what seemed like a long time through the opacity of his glasses. Then, as if reading her mind, he removed them.

"So, Tamara," he said. "How are you?"

Tamara liked his eyes. They were straightforward brown eyes with a twinkle of confidence.

"Nice office, Ted," she said, ignoring the question.

"You know," he said, "you are not at all as I pictured you."

"Really?" Tamara responded, intrigued. "And how was that?"

"Well, you look so, well, wholesome."

"Wholesome? Like I drink milk or something?"

"Kind of," he said. "Kind of healthy."

"Thanks," Tamara said tersely. "My daddy always told me, with his brains and my body I could write my own ticket."

"Nice guy," Ted said. "Rocket scientist?"

"Journalist."

"Hah," he laughed. "Lucky you."

"Yeah, only one thing more screwed up than a writer— a writer's brat. See, Ted," she added, suddenly serious, "I don't need an editor. I need a shrink. Will you be my shrink?"

"Tamara," he laughed, "I'm not a psychiatrist."

"I don't care," Tamara said. "I like you. I want to talk to you. I'd even pay you."

He raised his eyebrows.

"You don't have to pay me, Tamara," he said quietly. "I enjoy listening to you. I think you're fascinating."

"Really? Why's that?" Tamara urged desperately.

"Need you ask?" Ted replied, holding up a gray folder, presumably containing her story, and raising an eyebrow.

Tamara found herself breathing more quickly. The paper-filled room was rising around her, spinning. Flattery always hit her like that. It was like Jack Daniels, only better. She felt high. She sat back for a moment, getting her bearings.

Ted's office was pregnant with the ensuing silence. Tamara felt herself surrounded by it, comforted. She could hear the shallow pattern of her own quick breathing, the long slow pattern of his. She squeezed her eyes tightly shut and opened them quickly. Ted was watching her, a smile tugging at the muscular edges of his mouth.

"Tamara," he said. "You're quite an extraordinary person. I'm really glad that I've met you."

He got up, walked around the desk, and sat on the edge of it, right in front of her. Her face was eye-level with his lap. "Hey," he said, looking down at her, hands on his knees, his gaze direct, empathetic, penetrating. Tamara felt dizzy. His loins were a few inches away from her face. They were large and compelling—an all-powerful masculine vortex. In another few moments she was going to

Linda Watanabe McFerrin

collapse toward them. "Save me, Jesus," she thought. She needed a drink or something.

"Want to go for that drink now?" Ted asked, innocently reading her mind. "You talk. I listen. How does that sound?"

"Fine. It sounds fine," Tamara croaked huskily.

"Great!" Ted pulled her up from the chair. "Let's go, sweetheart," he said with a Bogie-like whistle of s's, and grabbed his jacket.

"Watch your step, here, Tamara," he directed, as he steered her through the archipelago of manuscripts that littered the floor. "It's not entirely safe."

"That's for sure," Tamara said looking over at him, drunk with proximity and desire.

He pivoted quickly in the carpeted hall. "Stairs or elevator?" he demanded. "Your choice."

"Oh, I don't care," Tamara said, back in rubber time again. "Whichever's slower."

The Hand of Buddha

Everything changed the day the Buddha's hand arrived in the mail. To Tess it was an unexpected miracle, because her life was beset with tribulation. That tribulation seemed to have begun months before when Norwood, her father, died—small and shrunken—his once-powerful body riddled with cancer. But really it had started almost a year before that when Jessica, Tess's mother and Norwood's wife, began to clearly exhibit the signs of her dementia. Neat little Jessica, who had always exercised a rigorous control over all of their lives, seemed suddenly to have cracked. She baked cookies and pies without adding flour, began taking baths with all of her clothes on, walked off the deck without using the stairs, and said strange things like, "I'm going to tomato the day. Will you join me?"

Norwood, frightened by his wife's sudden fall from perfection, took Jessica to the doctor. The doctor recommended a specialist who, in turn, recommended a clinic. Jessica was tested and questioned by a panel of nurses, psychologists, and neurologists who eventually reached a medical consensus: Jessica had Alzheimer's disease. That was when Norwood started to shrink. He grew pale and withdrew, shutting himself up in their home. He quit going fishing. He quit playing golf. When his poker pals called to invite him over, he'd say, "No, Jessica's not feeling well tonight. I'm going to stay in with her." And from his big chair in front of the TV, he watched Jessica cut pieces of kleenex into hundreds of tiny squares. He watched her take all the clothing out of the dressers and arrange them in piles on the living room floor. He watched her examine and carefully remove every leaf on the ficus, the dumb cane, the split-leaf philodendrons—on all of the houseplants that dotted the large rooms of their home with green.

Jessica, on the other hand, was oblivious to the changes in Norwood. She was busy hiding her jewelry in envelopes sequestered under chair cushions and pillows, busy brushing her hair with a toothbrush, busy pulling the flowers from each and every plant in the garden as soon as the blossoms appeared.

And Tess was also remiss, because even though she noted the subtle changes in Norwood when she visited her parents' home in Marina Del Mar, it was Jessica's condition that worried her most, and she would ask Norwood questions like when was the last time he'd taken Jessica to the doctor and was he feeding her enough leafy greens.

By the time Tess realized that something was terribly wrong with her father, it was too late. Norwood knew all along that he had some serious physical problems, but he tried to ignore them.

Linda Watanabe McFerrin

He was pacing himself against his wife's illness, trying to time his departure to roughly match up with hers. But his cancer was faster than her madness, and he beat her to the final checkpoint. This had not been a part of his plan.

He could barely speak in the hospital—he was too weak, but Tess could sense the frustration he felt about not completing his mission. In fact, the only word Norwood did manage to say as he lay there dying was "Jessica," and he said this not to Jessica, but to Tess. Tess thought that her father, delirious, had mistaken her for her mother, which in some ways was correct. If Norwood could have spoken, he would have said something like, "like mother, like daughter," or "the apple doesn't fall far from the tree."

Norwood died within a week of his admission into the same hospital that he visited with Jessica for her bimonthly checkups. Then, all too quickly it seemed, his ashes were scattered off the southern California coast as he had arranged, the house in Marina Del Mar was closed and locked up, and Jessica went home with Tess.

It had always been Jessica's way to change people's lives, even before her illness. Her dementia only compounded the effect. It didn't take long for Tess's world to unravel. Jessica paced the long hallways of Tess's house, never sleeping. She applied all of the strength in her ninety-pound frame to the boxes that Tess loaded with books and stacked in columns in front of the stairwells every night. Tess did this as a precaution. After all, Jessica had taken a tumble from the deck at the house in Marina del Mar; the same thing could happen again. Tess imagined her mother falling down the stairs that led into the darkness that pooled in the parlors under the bedrooms, and she couldn't sleep. Her ears and mind wandered with Jessica all through the house. Tess had draped bells over Jessica's doorknob so that she could keep track of her ramblings. Sometimes, as she listened, she thought of Norwood with his insomniac wife in that house in Marina Del Mar, how he must have chased her disease through the dream-starved corridors, his cancer loping along beside him.

By the time Norwood died and she moved in with Tess, Jessica's agitation had attained nearly supernatural levels. She was frail and had become very clumsy, but she never stopped moving. She fell in the bathroom. She fell on the stairs. She broke a finger and sprained her ribs. Tess spent several yellow-gray dawns perched uncomfortably on one or another of the green plastic chairs of the hospital emergency room. The doctors told her that the behavior was normal for someone with Jessica's illness. They suggested that Jessica walk with a cane.

Tess was trying to manage the crisis. Her business, her home, and her social commitments had always seemed to enjoy a precarious balance, one that she had to watch closely to avoid upsetting. All of a sudden, she was a juggler with one too many pins in the air. One by one, the carefully choreographed elements

Linda Watanabe McFerrin

of her life hit the dirt. She missed meetings, canceled projects, lost clients. Jessica seemed to defy all Tess's attempts to deftly handle the problem. In the course of two months, she went through twenty home-care professionals. She was expelled from three Alzheimer's and dementia daycare programs. She'd been given a cane which she rapidly learned to use as a weapon. She also used it as a tool with which to effect her escapes.

Meanwhile, Tess was losing patience and weight. Perpetually tired, she found herself scolding her mother.

"You have to stop driving them off," she pleaded.

But Jessica only sobbed and clung to her daughter. "I don't like them. They're turtles," she said abjectly. "Oh, Laura, Laura, you are the only one."

That's how things stood when the Buddha's hand arrived. The hand was a gift from Sirena La, the ethereal proprietress of the Wu Li Spring Garden, a tea shop and apothecary in La Jolla. Sirena specialized in herbal cures and magical brews like sea goddess broth, a blend of dry abalone, lichee, lily bulb, and lotus seed that she'd learned to mix from her ancestors, barefoot healers in the mountain villages of Vietnam. Sirena was one of Tess's clients, and when she became aware of Tess's dilemma, she felt a helping hand was in order. So she selected her present with care, carefully placing it in a white box wrapped in iris-colored tissue. Then, wielding her Mont Blanc pen as if it were the most delicate of sumi brushes, she composed a note.

Dear Tess,

How saddened I was to hear of your father's death and your mother's illness. No wonder I haven't heard from you! I am sending you my love and the Buddha's hand. The Buddha's hand will stay fresh for a very long time, but it is sweetest when used right away. Do not wait too long.

Take care,
Sirena

Tess was surprised by the messengered arrival of a package from Sirena addressed to her home. Opening the box, she peeled back the deep purple paper. A citrusy fragrance wafted into the air. In the box was a peculiar, lemon-colored fruit. It was the size of a hand, or more precisely, two hands folded in a prayer position. From the quarter-inch stem at the top of the fruit, ten root-shaped fingers extended, kissing at the tips; two of them, shorter than the rest, pressed side by side like a pair of perfect thumbs.

Tess felt overwhelmed by Sirena's kindness. For the first time in months, tears came to her eyes.

As for the fruit, she was not quite sure what to do with it, but it was so very strange and beautiful that the last thing she wanted to do was eat it. So she took it into the kitchen, where the latest home-care professional was preparing a lunch tray for

Linða Watanabe McFerrin

Jessica, and placed it in a celadon-colored bowl and put the bowl on top of the refrigerator.

Tess was just sliding it back toward the center of the surface when she heard the singing. It was coming from the table at which Jessica was seated, waiting for lunch. Jessica had never appeared much enamored with music, but suddenly, sitting there at the breakfast-room table, she started to belt out old tunes. First she sang personalized versions of "The Battle Hymn of the Republic" and "Amazing Grace." Then she sang "Yankee Doodle," making up words and padding around them with "ta-ta-ta-ta-tum-tum" and "tum-tum macaroni!"

"And here is your lunch, Jessica," the home-care professional said, sweetly enough, fooled, no doubt, by Jessica's singing. And Jessica hit her with the cane.

Of course, the home-care professional quit—number twenty-one in the rapidly lengthening series. And Tess, already exhausted, was faced with another dilemma.

"Oh, Mother, can't you see how hard you are making this for me," Tess wailed, tears streaming down her cheeks for the second time in one day. She had forgotten all about the Buddha's hand, which had been stopped mid-slide on its journey to the center top of the refrigerator, and which could be seen, lemony fingertips peeking over the rim of the celadon bowl.

"What? I've done nothing wrong. I never touched her," Jessica insisted sincerely. "You know I would never hurt you." Then she, too, started to cry.

It must have been sometime during those tears, or maybe it was during Jessica's quick burst of song, that the message was left on Tess's recorder.

"Hello, Tess, I'm Brother Fitzhugh of the Bodhisattva Fellowship; I'm a friend of Sirena La's. Sirena mentioned that you might be looking for a caregiver, and I want to recommend someone. Her grandfather is a personal acquaintance, a pastor at the Tonga Temple of Light Church. His granddaughter is lovely. She's done this type of work before. Her name is Ollalie . . ."

Tess did not have time to listen to the rest of the message because Jessica had decided to color her palms with lipstick. She was singing again, too, wobbling her way down the hall, cane in one hand, the other reaching out now and then to press its red palm into the wall for stability. It didn't take Tess long to dial for Ollalie. Jessica was still singing when Ollalie arrived.

Ollalie was Tess's last hope. She was a beautiful young woman from Tonga, with dark brown eyes and thick hair that rippled like a waterfall all the way down to the small of her back. Jessica took to Ollalie at once. "Open up your pearly gates," Jessica warbled. "California, here I come."

Ollalie thought Jessica was an angel. "No problem," she responded to Tess's interview questions. "I can take care of Grandma!" Then she laughed, and to Tess her laughter sounded like the wind stirring palm fronds or water dancing over pebbles and rocks; there was something elemental about it.

Linda Watanabe McFerrin

Ollalie arrived for her first day of work in a white 1981 Cadillac Seville with wire-spoke wheels, plenty of chrome, and a burgundy tuck-and-roll leather interior. It belonged to her grandfather, the pastor of the Tonga Temple of Light Church; Ollalie used it to run all of his errands. It's possible, in fact, that Ollalie considered Jessica one of his errands, or one of "His" errands as her grandfather liked to emphasize.

Tess and Jessica were both waiting anxiously in the front parlor for Ollalie's arrival. Jessica had earlier used her cane on the high front-door latch and managed to bolt toward the verandah steps before Tess noticed her missing. If Jessica hadn't stopped to pluck most of the new blossoms from the wisteria that wound its way through the verandah railings along the way, Tess would never have caught up with her, and Jessica would probably have launched herself over the top stair and into the void. Tess ushered Jessica back inside, locked the door, and collapsed into one of the armchairs. Jessica stood at the window and scratched at it, humming and swaying to the music she made. She wanted to go outside.

"Oh, let's go," she whined. Then she hummed for a while. "Let's go. Let's go," she chanted softly, swaying from side to side. The long fingernails on her thin-fingered hands scratched at the glass of the window.

When Jessica saw Ollalie pull up in the enormous white automobile she was overwhelmed with inexplicable joy. Still chewing on tunes, she hurried to the front door again, pounding upon it with all the force in her weakling frame. She crooned a greeting to Ollalie when Tess opened the door, and reaching into a pocket she pulled out a wisteria blossom and put it in Ollalie's hair.

Ollalie laughed her wonderful watery laugh, and Tess had to steady herself. She was certain they'd all been transported to Tonga.

"Grandma," Ollalie exclaimed, her eyes sparkling like round beads of jet, "you were waiting for me!"

"I did wait. Oh, yes. I knew you would come," Jessica answered, delighted. "Let's go," she chanted gently. Then she burst into song. "Whoa," said Jessica, "Whoa-ho, ho, ho, ho," getting ready to bound down the stairs.

Ollalie, who spent most of her time on her grandfather's missions, soon began to take Jessica with her on all of "His" errands.

Jessica, sitting next to Ollalie, barely able to see over the top of the option-loaded dash, pinned by her safety belt to her seat in the vast, tucked-leather interior of the minister's car, would sing out the names on the road signs. "Felix Road. Old Tucker Expressway," she reported with real pleasure.

"That's right, Grandma," Ollalie would answer, turning into the wide drive of the Temple of Light to deliver her grandfather's lunch.

Meanwhile, Tess was dreaming about Tonga. She wanted to board a plane or a boat and end up in the South Pacific. Norwood had at one time traveled all over the South Pacific.

He'd been there during the Second World War. He'd been to the Solomon Islands, to New Caledonia, and he'd been to the Coral Sea. Later, when he was not such a young man, he'd gone back on his own. He loved to tell Tess stories about it. He went back, he said, because of the beauty. On that trip, he visited Fiji, American Samoa, and an island called Rarotonga. Tess wondered all of a sudden if Norwood had built the house in Marina Del Mar so that he could stare out over the vast expanse of the Pacific, out past the clockwork sunsets toward those islands . . . and she wondered if, when his ashes were scattered, there, off the coast as he had arranged, if the winds had grabbed them and carried them off to some quiet cove or coral reef that he had discovered decades before.

At Tess's request Ollalie loaned her a book about Tonga. The book was about His Majesty Taufa'ahau Tupou IV of the Kingdom of Tonga. On the cover of the book was a photograph of a very large man in white gloves and a white parade jacket. The man's chest was covered with medals, his eyes in sunglasses. A direct descendant of King George Tupou I, who is considered the founder of modern Tonga, this king was the son of her late Majesty Queen Salote Tupou III. Tess studied the picture closely. The man had a sash over his very wide chest and another around his big waist. His jacket sported gold-braided epaulettes, and he stood in front of a venetian blind. Tess tried to imagine him laughing. He must, she determined, have a laugh like waves crashing against a rocky shore, like thunder rumbling before a monsoon.

Tess decided she wanted to go and stay on the "Friendly Islands," as the Islands of Tonga are sometimes called. She would eat coconut and bananas and sweet potatoes and taro. She would pick breadfruit and feel the rough, wet sand gathering in between her toes. She was certain her laughter, too, would rise up over the coral limestone of the 170 islands of Tongatapu, Ha'apai and Vava'u. It would ring through the volcanoes that climb from the ocean depths like the clapper inside a bell.

"Do you go back to Tonga often?" Tess asked Ollalie, wanting to know more about the young woman's birthplace.

"Oh, yes," Ollalie answered, one arm around Jessica's shoulders. Jessica was nibbling on an Eskimo Pie. "But not that often; it's very expensive."

"I'd like to go," said Tess, watching the thin chocolate shell of the eskimo pie collapse under the pressure of Jessica's lips. "I'd like to go to Tonga one day."

With Ollalie's help, Tess was getting her life back on track. She was catching up with her work again. She was finally getting some sleep. But she was not the business woman she once was. Her interest wandered. It was as if she'd been swept away by a swift new current. The current was pulling her toward Tonga.

Sometimes she'd watch Jessica tottering about in the yard, Ollalie at her side, as she plucked the new blooms off the azaleas, the young lemons off their bushes. Sometimes a long line of neighborhood children trailed her like a bridal veil. Jessica

Linda Watanabe McFerrin

gave them flowers and lemons. Since Ollalie arrived, Jessica, out all the time, had been befriended by the neighborhood children. It was summertime, and, like Jessica, the children had nothing to do but play.

"Can Jessica come out and play?" they would ask when they came knocking at the door.

"Yes, yes, of course," Tess always said.

"Can we have some more lemons?" they'd ask slyly.

"Yes, yes, of course," Tess would respond.

A flow had definitely come into Tess's life. Very different from her old juggling act, which consisted of tightly defined projects and carefully timed execution, this flow was made up of the daily interactions of Jessica, Tess, and Ollalie, of the comings and goings of the white 1981 Cadillac Seville, of flowers, streams of neighborhood children, and the scent of freshly picked lemons. Ollalie had only been with them for a little over a month, and already her generous and effortless ways were transforming Tess's world. Tess had time to think. She had time to visit several private-care residences in the hope that she would find the perfect match for her mother. She had time for Jessica, and strangely, for once in her life, she also had time for herself. Sometimes she thought of this as island magic. More often she thought of it simply as the grace of gifts, of the power of care, symbolized by the two golden hands joined in prayer which had turned, in her mind, into a kind of shrine in the celadon bowl on top of the refrigerator.

But the dictates of Jessica's illness proved powerful, too.

One day Ollalie approached Tess, her eyes shiny with tears. "I'm so sorry, Tess," she said. "I cannot work for you anymore."

"But why?" Tess asked, astonished.

"It's Grandma," Ollalie replied. "She doesn't want me anymore."

Tess could see, just by looking at Ollalie, that this disclosure was painful to her, but she had to press on with some questions. She had to get the whole story, and she knew that she wouldn't get it from Jessica.

"Ollalie, Ollalie," Tess said, tenderly patting the young woman's back, her hand almost getting tangled up in the dark waterfall of tresses, "I know this is difficult for you; it's hard for me, too. Can you tell me what happened?"

"Well," sniffed Ollalie, wiping her eyes on the spotless, white handkerchief that Tess had so kindly proffered, "Jessica try to get into someone else's car this morning. She climb into the car and say, 'let's go,' and no one can get her out. The other people in the car really need to leave, so I tell Jessica that she has to get out of the car. 'Jessica,' I say, 'please come out,' then I give her my hand to help her out."

At this point Ollalie's lovely, full lips quivered and altered their shape. They bowed downward, and her whole face seemed to fall with them. Tears flooded her eyes once more and cascaded from them, tears as elemental as her laughter, a great torrent soaking the handkerchief, carrying Tess, Jessica, hope, away from them.

Linda Watanabe McFerrin

"Then Jessica grab my hair," Ollalie continued. "She grab my hair, and she pull it, and she tell me she don't like me anymore, and then she slap my face, hard."

Tess could feel the slap on Ollalie's face as if it were on her own. The slap that rocked the friendly isles and sent them down to the bottom of the sea. "Oh, Ollalie, I'm sorry," she said.

"So, Grandma don't love me anymore, and I can't work for you," Ollalie sputtered, tears splashing down her cheeks.

"Yes, I see. Yes, Ollalie, I understand," Tess heard herself saying as Ollalie retrieved her purse from the coat closet.

"I finally get Jessica to come out of the car," Ollalie added sorrowfully. "The people were very angry. Jessica is resting inside now," she concluded, pointing toward the wide pocket doors of one of the parlors.

"Do you want to say goodbye?" Tess asked, feeling helpless.

"No," said Ollalie, head bowed, cheeks still wet with tears. "Grandma don't want to see me."

"Oh, I think she probably does," Tess added, escorting Ollalie toward the front door. "Will you come back and visit?"

"Yes," Ollalie nodded. "Yes, I will," she promised, walking out of their lives, and Tess, sighing heavily, bolted the door behind her and turned to the parlor.

Jessica was seated in the parlor in the big, wingback chair—her favorite—with her thin legs held straight out in front of her.

"Look," said Jessica, merrily glancing up from admiring her skinny limbs, smoothing the paper-thin flesh with her hands.

"These are such nice pencils. Aren't they nice pencils, Peggy?"

"Yes, very nice," Tess answered sadly. She realized with a pang that she loved most things about Jessica, and those wiry little appendages were no exception. "Yes, they are lovely pencils, Mother. But tell me, what exactly happened with Ollalie?"

"Oh, I don't know, that girl is crazy," said Jessica, and something in her voice made Tess realize that at some level she did know, and that like Ollalie, Jessica, too, was ready to break into tears.

"Well, darling, who really knows anything, anyway?" Tess soothed, perching on the arm of the wingback chair and wrapping one arm around Jessica. She thought, again, of the Buddha's hand in the celadon bowl in the kitchen. It had begun to look a little old, a bit sun-scorched, like a hand that had started to tan. Tess mentally counted the days that Ollalie had been with them. Forty-three days. That's how long it had been. It was forty-three days ago that she had received Sirena's gift. She wondered if she could still eat it, if the fruit could still be enjoyed.

"Let's go to the kitchen, and I'll make you a snack," Tess said to Jessica, helping her out of the chair. The Buddha's hand, she concluded, was quite old already and possibly very bitter. She had definitely waited too long. But that was all right, it needn't be perfect. She would try it anyway. She would enjoy it, too, even if all it had was a trace of the old sweetness.

Tess walked to the kitchen with her arm around Jessica's shoulders. Jessica was making music again, humming happily to herself.

Linda Watanabe McFerrin

"It's just us again. You and me," Tess whispered into her mother's ear, thinking of a particular private-care residence that she had visited, a very expensive one, one that reminded her of a resort. It was staffed with a host of Ollalies.

"But right now we are going to have a treat. First, I am going to give you an Eskimo Pie," Tess said, reaching into the freezer and liberating the chocolate and vanilla delicacy from its wrapper.

"Then I am going nibble into this delectably odd piece of fruit," she added, taking the Buddha's hand down off the top of the refrigerator and removing it from the celadon bowl in which it had been enshrined. "I am not going to wait any longer. Sour or sweet, I am going to enjoy it. And I am going to enjoy it all.

"And last, but not least," Tess concluded, grabbing the phone and tucking it under one arm as she pulled the phone book, left-handed, from its place on the pantry shelf, the Buddha's hand still held in her right hand, "I am going to ring up the first travel agent that I find in the phone book, and I'm going to purchase two tickets to Tonga. There you go, Mother," she laughed, "what do you think of that?"

"Yum," said Jessica, getting ready to fill her mouth with Eskimo Pie. "Yum, yum, yum."

How to Fall in Love

This is how you fall in love: you need a full moon and a snow-covered, high mountain wilderness. You need an ice-blue winter meadow dotted with run-down cabins, a boyfriend who calls you "butter bean" for no apparent reason, and you need a stranger.

That was Jennifer's recipe—a special alchemical process combining unlikely elements, and like any alchemical process, this one was ultimately a feat of discovery and a matter of revelation.

"Look, butter bean," Andy announced one Wednesday night at dinner a few weeks after they'd met through Missy Trudeau's Dating Service, "I have a plan for a brilliant weekend."

"Butter bean." That name, Jennifer thought, did not suit her at all. She was tough and well-muscled, hardly a butter bean. She wondered how Andy had come up with that name. It must have been a generic nickname that he applied to all of his girl-friends. She was, she concluded, one in a series of butter beans.

"Jennifer, are you listening to me?" he asked, noting the far-away look on her face.

It was a small face haloed with lovely blonde curls. Missy Trudeau had certainly done him a service.

"Jennifer, do you want to hear more about this brilliant idea?"

"Yes," Jennifer answered. "Sure, Andy. Of course."

"I have this friend, Darby," Andy gushed in response. "You'll really love her, Jennifer. She's so much fun. Anyway, Darby's family has a cabin in Tahoe, in the high Sierra, in a place called Euer Valley. It's miles and miles of privately held cross-country ski runs. Darby's invited us up."

Andy wondered if he was, perhaps, trying too hard. He always seemed to do this with women. This, he thought, was what scared them away.

Jennifer was wondering if Darby was also a butter bean, an old or not-so-old girlfriend. She wasn't quite sure how to ask.

"Darby's an old girlfriend?" she observed, squinting so that her violet eyes looked extremely intense.

"Who? Darby?" Andy squeaked, unmanned by the dusty gold lashes that ringed those eyes. Then he caught Jennifer's drift. "Oh yes, she's an old friend. I've known her for years. She'll be going up with her boyfriend, Paul."

"Well, sure," Jennifer said cautiously, not caring to misstep in the familiar old pas de deux. "Sure, I'd love to go."

Jennifer hadn't given up yet on Andy. She was intrigued. So far, Andy seemed to exactly fit the requirements she had given to Missy Trudeau's service. She'd been around so many pouncers and bouncers, it was great to go out with a man who called her up and read poetry to her over the phone, a man with a real job.

"No! I am not Prince Hamlet, nor was meant to be;
Am an attendant lord, one that will do
To swell a progress, start a scene or two . . .

Shall I part my hair behind? Do I dare to eat a peach?
I shall wear white flannel trousers, and walk upon the beach.
I have heard the mermaids singing, each to each."

"Mmm," Jennifer had purred into the phone. "That's so nice."

"T. S. Eliot, Jennifer. One of my favorites."

"I really like it; it's so sensitive."

"Tentative?"

"No, sensitive."

"Well, thank you. T. S. really tells it like it is."

Andy was excited and pleased that Jennifer had decided to go up to Darby's cabin with him. He hadn't been up there in a while, and it was a beautiful place. Redwood, cedar, ponderosa, and a sugar pine perfumed the air. Dogwood berries blazed red where later white blossoms would float like small pats of butter scattered amid the green, baby leaves. Euer Meadow itself, high in the mountains, would still be covered with snow—the buttercups, poppies, and lupine not yet unveiled.

Andy had once had sex with Darby up at the cabin. He had wonderful memories of a couple of nights with hurricane lamps and blue spatter-tin bowls full of cornflakes, peaches, and thick condensed milk. Just the two of them stoking the wood burning stove, Darby laughing, telling him he should begin with the soft wood, the pine, then add oak for a long slow burn, the kind you can count on. It was a fling. They were really so wrong for each other. But it was fun, and he was always glad to be up at the cabin again.

Jennifer felt her entire being unlock as they headed up into the mountains. Her chest seemed to unbutton and the wild world rushed in. Gone were her email directives to Pacific Rim plants that always seemed to misinterpret instructions. Gone were the slow and endlessly ineffectual committees on which she was forced to serve. Gone were the office, the computers, the secretary who persisted in doing just as she pleased in spite of the bad reviews Jennifer gave her, in spite of the meetings with personnel.

In their place were soft catspaw and silvery snowbrush, the fuzzy-friendly red bark of giant sequoias and flaming wands of Indian paintbrush.

At 5,000 feet, they still hadn't seen snow. Spring had set itself up like a fair in the foothills, waving foxtail fans and green pennants of foliage. The late afternoon sun glanced off round hills, slid into the gullies between them.

At 6,000 feet, cliffs walled the road that climbed into mountains. They began to see patches of dirty gray ice, ectoplasmic scraps clinging to small spots of shadow. The line of blue mountain, bonnetted in white, shouldered closer.

At 7,000 feet, sheets of black ice covered the roadway in places. It was getting dark. Andy switched the jeep into four-

Linda Watanabe McFerrin

wheel drive. They had moved several months back in time, back to winter. The thick carpet of white, many feet deep, lay profound and impregnable.

They came upon Euer Valley by moonlight. It was diamond-bright in the cold night light. Cedars looked almost blue against star-dotted skies, pines like Chinese hermits bearded in white.

At the meadow's edge Darby's family cabin twinkled like a rustic reindeer harnessed in white Christmas tree lights. A narrow road cut through the four-foot-deep snow toward it. This was the only artery upon the otherwise unbroken surface.

"God, that's beautiful," Andy whistled into the darkness.

"Mmm," Jennifer murmured, tearing her eyes from the vista to glance at his shadowy profile. She was getting used to the moments of aesthetic perfection that she seemed to stumble into with Andy.

They approached at a crawl along the skinny drive ermined in snow. The cabin seemed to get smaller as they approached. Snow crunched under their boots as they moved toward the porch, carefully taking the ice-covered steps.

"Come on in. It's open," came the quick response to a knock.

It was frosty inside the cabin, and it smelled of lamp oil, leather, and Murphy's oil soap.

The man had just risen out of his seat, an armchair of saddle-brown leather surrounded by books.

"Hi," he said, extending a hand in a fast, easy movement.

"Like drawing a gun from a holster," Jennifer thought.

"Harrison. Darby's dad," the man said. "Just had a girl here to clean." Perhaps he had noticed Jennifer's affinity for the Murphy's oil smell.

"Hi, Harry," Andy said. "My name's Andy."

A series of three little bells rang in Jennifer's body. Harrison was tall and lanky, a wiry sixty- or seventy-something. He had a horseman's hand; that hand spoke in its way. He seemed to hear what she was thinking.

Jennifer warmly returned the handshake. "Jennifer," she said with a nod.

A big smile spread over Harry's lined face.

"There's a couple of steaks and some beer in the fridge if you kids are hungry," he announced. "Help yourselves. Sleeping bags? You have something to sleep in?"

"In the car," Andy answered.

"Okay," Harry said. "You two sleep in here."

"I'll be out on the porch if you need me," he added, stuffing a pack of Marlboro cigarettes into his front shirt pocket. "Darby won't let me smoke inside when she has guests up," he explained. "Slows me down, but it doesn't stop me."

"Just make yourselves comfortable," he added lightly. "The cabin isn't big, but it's homey."

"It is more than homey. It's perfect," Jennifer thought, as she opened cupboards and helped Andy stow their gear. Her daydreams were set in cabins like this one. It was movie-set special. There were pictures of cowboys and cowgirls up on the walls and oil lamps in the rooms. There was rat poison under the sink.

Linda Watanabe McFerrin

Jennifer and Andy pan-fried steaks by the moonlight streaming in through the kitchen window. They lit hurricane lamps. Andy opened two bottles of beer.

"That Harry is a character," Jennifer said with undisguised admiration.

"Yep," Andy agreed. "A real Marlboro Man."

Harry hung out on the porch, smoking, for a very long time. Then Andy and Jennifer heard a door slam, an engine start, and a pickup truck move quickly away from the cabin. Soon enough they were passed out in sleeping bags on the living room floor. They didn't hear Harry return later that night, but the next morning at daybreak Jennifer heard him as he tried to tiptoe past their recumbent forms, heading outside again.

She bolted from bed and caught him at the door.

"Where are you going, Harry?" she asked, sounding like a six-year-old kid about to be left behind.

Harry took a good long look at the young woman in the T-shirt and the big woolen socks. She had a mane of yellow-gold hair, lean, well-formed limbs, big feet and hands. "Listen," he said kindly, "I'm going to do chores. Tonight you and Andy sleep in my room. Darby and Paul will be here later today. They'll take the living room floor."

"Hey, that's great," Jennifer said, suddenly thinking that her legs must look mighty thin where they disappeared into the wide mouths of her socks. "But what about you?"

"Kitchen, maybe," Harry laughed. "Make pancakes this morning," he added. "Use plenty of syrup. Snowshoes and skis are in the back." Then he reached around her and gave her a hug, a big grizzly hug that reminded her of sleeping bags and woolly mittens when the windchill is low.

"Harrison Raley, whoa," she thought. "I could fall in love with you."

Jennifer made the pancakes and covered them with plenty of syrup just as Harry had dictated. Harry was right to suggest them. Andy said that he'd rather have cornflakes if they could find them in the cupboard. They found them. Watching Andy pour milk over the cereal, Jennifer considered that she might have preferred cornflakes too, if Harrison hadn't planted the pancake seed. After breakfast they grabbed the snowshoes and trekked out to the forest, leaving the meadow unmarred. They would share that with Darby when she got to the cabin.

Darby still hadn't arrived when they got back. When she finally showed up, she wasn't with Paul. A friend whom she introduced as Cecelia was with her. Cecelia had freckles and fiery red tresses.

"Hi, Darby," Andy greeted his old pal with a kiss. "Hello, Cecelia," he said with a sweet, boyish smile.

"Will this be the next butter bean?" Jennifer wondered with a pang.

"This darling lass is Jennifer," Andy proudly announced, his smile banishing all other butter beans past and future.

Linda Watanabe McFerrin

"Hi, Jennifer," Darby said. Cecelia shook Jennifer's hand.

"Where is Harrison, anyway?" Darby demanded with some impatience.

"I'm right here, Darby," Harry said, stepping up to the porch behind her. "Where's Paul?"

"We had a fight," Darby snapped, spinning around to address her father, eyes shooting daggers. "Harry, this place just gets smaller and smaller."

"Maybe it does," said Harry. "Or, maybe you just get bigger and bigger. I'm sorry to hear you two had a fight."

"His fault, of course," said Darby.

"Of course," Harry nodded and smiled. "Well, I've got some wood to stack," he told them. Then he headed back down to the steps.

"Let me help you, Harry," Andy offered.

"No, no, you kids go skiing—it's perfect cross-country weather. Darby, you haven't been here all year. Got some oak for you this time, Darby," he hollered at the house, leaping into his pickup where the new wood was stacked.

"Just look at him," Darby grumbled. "Mr. Macho. He just never stops."

"Harry seems like a cool dude to have for a dad," Jennifer observed.

Darby gave her a withering look. "Well, let's unload our stuff, and let's ski," she said. "Harry told us to ski, so we will."

It was yet another brilliant idea, Jennifer thought. The day was perfect for skiing—so warm and bright that they could wear swimming-suit tops and sunglasses and had to cover themselves in sunscreen.

"What's Darby's problem?" Jennifer asked Andy, as they shushed along after their hostess and her pal.

"She's cranky because of the fight with Paul," Andy offered.

"Probably," Jennifer agreed.

Whatever the reason, Darby's bad mood wore off. Soon they were all laughing and having a great time. When they got back to the cabin, Harry's pickup was empty, all the wood stacked on a pallet. Harry was dressed up in jeans and a starched, button-down shirt. He was wearing a cowboy hat, too.

"All you youngsters being around," he began, "I've got a colt kicking up its heels inside me. I'm heading for Tahoe," he continued, "for some fun and some luck. Wish it to me," he demanded.

"Good luck, Dad," Darby said. "Maybe one day those cards will listen to you."

"I keep trying to get through," Harry said soulfully. "I just need to find the right language."

Then he left in his pickup truck with the silver stallion hood ornament.

"He's going to meet some gal there in Tahoe," Darby said with a tone of disgust. "Such a jerk sometimes," she added with a faint frown in her eyes.

Jennifer wondered about Darby's mother—who she was, how she fit into the picture. Darby looked, after all, just like Harrison.

Linda Watanabe McFerrin

She was tall and lanky, deeply tanned, with the same head of cocoa-brown hair, although Harry's was streaked with gray.

"Andy, go get that bag," Darby was saying, peremptorily pointing to a big paper sack on her father's leather chair. "We brought up the mixings for some fine margaritas."

She sounded like Harrison, too, Jennifer decided. Who could argue with her? The drinks were another good Raley idea.

They made three blenders full of margaritas, experimenting with various combinations of tequila, triple sec, and lime juice. By the time they had the proportions worked out they were looped, especially Darby, who drank with a real sense of purpose.

Cecelia mashed avocados. Jennifer opened two big jars of double-star salsa.

Andy stepped them through the preparation of sizzling chicken fajitas.

They munched and drank and talked about life, about jobs and futures and dead-end relationships. They even talked about hope, Jennifer singing Andy's praises, although she couldn't help thinking about Darby's dad.

"Remember that poem, Andy?" she said fondly. "What was that poem? Say it again, okay?"

"Oh, boy, poetry," Darby said sourly. "Talk about lovebirds. You two are pretty sickening."

Jennifer was getting just a little bit tired of Darby's constant criticisms of everyone around her.

"Then there are people like me and Paul," Darby continued,

drunkenly flinging herself down on her dad's leather chair and drenching one of the arms in a margarita waterfall.

"We're like oil and water," she groaned. "You'd think we'd get along. We like the same things, behave the same way, but we just keep getting on each other's nerves. It's like two people trying to occupy the same space. You know, we both want to sleep on the left side of the bed. No one wants to give in. So we fight all the time. But the worst of it," she added, polishing off the rest of her drink and turning the glass upside down, "the worst of it is, that he kisses exactly like Harry."

The corners of Darby's mouth turned downward, as if she were going to cry—like the glass, like a horseshoe with all the luck running out.

Andy, Jennifer, and Cecelia exchanged looks of shock. Jennifer imagined Harrison kissing Darby—kissing the girl just like him. She felt herself shudder. Cecelia took Darby's arm, gently removing the upturned margarita glass from her hand. Darby sniffed twice. She was not going to cry. She rubbed the tip of her nose with the back of her hand.

"Cecelia," she said, getting out of the chair, "let's do one round of poppers, then go to bed. Okay, sweetie? Whadaya say? I'm tired."

Cecelia nodded and escorted Darby into the kitchen with a wide-eyed look back over her shoulder toward Andy and Jennifer.

"Sleep in Harry's bed," Jennifer called after them. She watched her voice float through the tight cabin toward the kitchen's

Linda Watanabe McFerrin

cramped entrance. "Andy and I will sleep on the living room floor."

"Whew," said Andy. "That was a surprise. I don't know about you, Jennifer, but my head is spinning from all the margaritas. How about a quick breather outside?"

"Yes," Jennifer said, her voice full of gratitude. "My head is in a whirl, too. Poor Darby," she whispered. "Poor Harry. Poor Paul."

She thought about Harrison one more time—smile on his rugged face, hands full of cards. She thought of all the other tough men she had loved. She took a deep breath and released the images, letting them all go, stepping with Andy out into the starlight.

Maʒai Heart

Red. Red. Red. The earth was an adamant Masai-red. And beneath the plane—opals and amethyst—the land was set with swimming pools and purple clouds of jacaranda.

Faith squinted out through the window of the Twin Otter as it purred over the Nairobi suburbs, the last edifices and constructs melting into the distance. How long had she been in Africa? Not long really, not long in the context of her life. Something about the continent fascinated her. And she was getting old anyway. Well, you only have one life. You really only get one chance.

She thought about her brother, Martin. He'd died as a child. And here she was, thirty-eight and unmarried, the last of her line.

"Last of the Mohicans," she'd joke brutally during introductions. "Last of the Mohicans," she whispered to the wing of the plane.

Moving out over the savanna, the land below was in ripples that looked like waves. And the road looked like a red string laid out upon it, curvilinear in some places, sharply angled in others. It was good to look down on the road.

A few days earlier she had been on it, heading south from Mount Kenya with Philip. "What's your real name?" she asked between bites of sugar cane. "I don't want to call you Philip."

"My African name is Mungai," Philip had answered sheepishly. "My Christian name is Philip."

"Well, I'm going to call you Mungai," Faith asserted, spitting the sugar cane fiber, sucked dry, into her palm and tossing it out the window of the moving car, onto the side of the road.

She had called him Mungai after that with some effort. But in her head, he was still Philip. She couldn't change that. Her mind just persisted with Philip.

Later, in Nairobi, just before she boarded the plane, when they had lunch at a horrible, smoky place that Faith suspected was strictly for tourists, when she had tried to acquaint Philip with her philosophy regarding the vanity of souvenirs, he grew suddenly terribly thoughtful. "You Americans are clever people," he said.

Faith read "clever" as "tricky," as if she were trying to outsmart him. Philip said this because he didn't quite trust her. He said it because he was Kikiyu. A Masai, Faith reflected, would never have said something like that. A Masai would have thought it and looked away. In Faith's mind, that was the difference between the two tribes. The Kikiyu wanted to understand. The Masai didn't care. They were content in the difference.

"It's a cultural thing, Mungai," Faith had explained as a waiter came by, proferring his skewer of roasted oryx. Faith shook her head "no." It was important to her that Philip under-

Linda Watanabe McFerrin

stand her culture, that he should see its purpose. She threw her weight into her explanation. "We have to be clever," she insisted, thinking of Moi, of the elections, groping for common ground. "We believe in self-determination. If you aren't clever, people take your freedom away."

Philip nodded. He'd understood. He was Kikiyu. To a Masai, her explanation wouldn't have mattered. A Masai would have laughed. No one can take Masai freedom away.

Yes, that was what Faith loved about the Masai. She was glad to be going back to the Mara.

The plane was flying over the grassland. The grassland was dotted with Masai villages. Their circular compounds, ringed in gray thornbush to keep out the big cats, looked like moles or freckles on the face of the plain. Spotted. Mara means spotted. Masai Mara, the Masai's spotted land. Semblances of road, rut-clogged arteries, meandered like rivers along the gentle slope of the tree-tufted hills where the grasslands seemed to advance like a big tide.

Thatch-roofed huts. Circular huts. Circular compounds. They think in circles here, Faith remembered.

She could hear her friend Charlotte telling her to pick a rune from the bag of stones just before she'd headed for Kenya. She put her hand into the bag and withdrew one. The stone was runeless, a blank. According to the book, it meant death.

"No, it's a new beginning," Charlotte had insisted, tossing her blonde hair. "That's what you need—a new beginning. Africa," she'd drawled, thinking black men, thinking South.

The plane wheezed suddenly, as if in response to that thought. Sputtered. The quadruple rows of dials in the cockpit, which Faith could see from her seat, appeared to go wild. The pilot's hands flew around for a moment in panic. Then the hiccup subsided just as quickly as it had erupted.

Beneath the aircraft the turf had turned velvety green, a green carpet dotted with trees, tall solitary trees, clustered only occasionally, as if by accident, as if in passing. Like the Masai—the herders and their cattle—the trees were migrating, moving along. Like the elephants, dirt-brown on the green plain. Like the crocodiles in the Mara river. Like the Masai warriors dressed in bright red.

Looking up, Faith saw the gray underbelly of the great white frigate clouds and higher still the clear blue—nearly white—pulled upward into nothingness.

They were selling their land into nothingness; selling their little ebony animals, row upon row; pouring the strength of the forest, its life, into the small wooden statues, fetishes riding the great commercial ark. What was it worth? What was it all worth, anyway?

Anything important is worth ending. That's what Keith had said two years ago when he left her, when everything started to go sour. Anyway, he was right. Anything important *was* worth ending.

Faith moved her attention to a point just outside the window. The plane had started to cough again, and the propeller attached to one of its engines had become visible, reminding her

Linda Watanabe McFerrin

that its power was all an illusion. It was, after all, just a careful piece of metal, twisted and torqued to certain alien specifications. Faith realized, with a start, that the plane was going to crash.

"Look," she prayed. "Not just now. Not with a belly full of meat." It seemed a nasty thing to go like that, somehow unclean.

The aircraft responded with a sloppy seesaw.

"As if," she snickered, "as if you can bargain with fate."

She watched the people around her unravel, watched them jump up like flames, climb the smoothly curved walls of the cabin. There's not a lot you can do, she thought irritably. Things were happening fast. The remaining span of their lives could probably be measured in seconds. Faith wasn't going to squander them. She wanted a glass of champagne.

"Last of the Mohicans," she muttered, as the plane plunged Mara-ward to meet the Kenyan earth in a goodbye kiss, the G-force making her smile, her eardrums exploding with sound.

Red.

Amphibians

The difficulty stemmed from the fact that she had married a fish. "A fish," that's what they called him—his sister, Daphne; his mother, Alice; his father, Clay. He was long-limbed and white, with slender feet like natural fins. He was fond of pointing out swimmers' feet.

"Look," he'd say admiringly, "Feet like paddles. He'll probably win."

And he was always right. A fish from a family of fish.

They swam. The whole darn family swam. Their lives revolved around the 165-foot, water-filled rectangle that was their pool. They ate there and drank there. They fought and made up there. When Alice had each of her babies, there was no need to study Leboyer or to give birth to her children in bathtubs. The water was always with her. She floated through life. She nursed her little ones through sunburns and ear infections, plucked them from the water when they started to fight, and toweled them dry when they started to shiver, their teeth chattering like baby castanets.

Melanie couldn't swim. She was afraid of the water, but she learned to live by the pool. When you marry a fish, the water is always a few feet away. Her complexion turned golden, then brown. Red highlights darted down the dark fall of her hair, and a light scattering of freckles cast itself over the bridge of her nose. To fit in, a nonswimmer among fish, she mastered certain deceptions. She learned to look languid, under the harsh sunlight, her book tented over her, while the boisterous family voices rose over the water. She learned to captivate Jake's father, Clay, the least zealous swimmer, and trap him in long conversations. She learned to smile and shake her head demurely when her Fish would glance over, raise his eyebrows, and suggest the watery pleasures of his domain. Sometimes she would sit at the edge of the pool and dangle a sylph-like leg in the water. Then her Fish would swim over. He'd leap up from the water to kiss her, pleased with himself, with the ease and facility of the movement. And Melanie would laugh, shake off the splash, and retreat from the pool. And he'd follow her, landed, transformed again into a gravity-governed creature. Melanie rarely slipped into the pool when the others were there. It was too risky. They were too careless, too casual about the water.

Her most vivid memory was of the pool in Medicine Bow. Children swarmed it like flies. She was one more fly in the heat. Her mother had said, distastefully, that the children peed in the pool, and that had quelled Melanie's ardor, so that she hung back when her father was teaching the boys how to swim. In school, she heard that polio came from the water. She thought of this every year when they lined up for the sugar cubes in small paper

Linda Watanabe McFerrin

cups, as the bitterness of the medicine crept down her throat and into her body. She thought about this when she saw the children with leg braces or anyone in a wheelchair. She thought of Franklin Delano Roosevelt swimming, as a child, through his long summers. And pools were linked, in her mind, with disease.

Still, the water threaded its way through her childhood. Swimming holes in Wyoming—the Milk River, the Snake—the boys' splashing dives into the murky green. They were beautiful memories. It was true that all of the moments in her life that approached perfection were somehow linked with water—that carefree, fluid dimension. But inextricably tangled with these were the pains—warnings about the slipperiness of the serpentine riverbeds (she pictured snakes in the mottled underwater green); a fall and a cut on sharp, hidden rocks; the fear of infection; later her own lumpish adolescent form in a swimsuit; and ultimately, and most frightening of all, her big brother's drowning in the cold waters of the Trinity Alps.

Fate has a way of dealing strange cards. She didn't know, when she met him, that Jake was a fish. When she found out, she was a little afraid, her eyes widening as Jake's mother, Alice, proudly pulled forth medal after medal. Jake was a North Coast Champion. He'd set multiple records in the hundred-meter individual medley. But that might have been part of the attraction—his mastery of a substance that made her flesh quake.

So her most perfect moments were still bound to the water and peppered with a generous helping of her fears. She could never move inland. She would always be a girl clinging desperately to flotsam, watching helplessly from the shore.

For their honeymoon, she and Jake had gone to Puerto Vallarta. The trip was a gift from Alice and Clay. Jake and the water were nearly inseparable. When Melanie looked into his blue eyes, she saw the sea. She combed the shoreline, growing sun-warmed and brown. Jake's fair skin, charmed by the latitude, turned rosy, then burned. His nose became bright as a strawberry, and his lips swelled and blistered. His eyelids, sun-damaged, were difficult to open, and he squinted through the gold fringe of his lashes. The sunglasses hurt the tender bridge of his nose. His sun-bleached hair was stiff and unkempt, painful to run a comb through, and his scalp turned the color of flame. Melanie bought him a Panama hat. She wrapped his long legs in the white gauze of her Indian cotton skirt. She remembered Alice's tales of her children's summers. How, ill-suited for sunshine, they would burn, and she would wrap them in Crisco and wax paper—the only thing to relieve the pain. Melanie pictured Alice's children lying like cookies on their thin twin beds. She dubbed Jake her "darling albino." Swathed in his white shirt and the filmy lap rug, he would sit like an invalid in the shade of the palms, sipping daquiris and waiting for nightfall. At night, he swam in the dark waters of the hotel pool or in the black, starlit waters of the sea. And Melanie watched and thought of a poem that her mother read to her when she was a child, ". . . we've gone to search for the herring fish that live in this beautiful sea. Nets of silver and gold have we . . ." Still she was afraid. When she took her eyes, momentarily, from the lone swimmer in the black sea to look down at her hands, she saw that she was wringing them and that her knuckles were white.

Jake coached water polo and managed a pool. He taught life-saving to crazy little kids. Every day he would swim his laps, and Melanie sometimes went to the pool to watch him. She loved to see him move through the water—effortless, fluid, like a magical thing—a seahorse, a porpoise, something half-man, half-fish. He was fast in the water, and powerful, flicking here and there like an eel. And when he rose, water streaming from him in the humid indoor natatorium, she would catch her breath quickly, grateful that once more he'd come back to her, and she could relax again.

Jake's skin smelled faintly of chlorine. He looked like a mad-man, his eyes rabbit-red. Melanie bought him new goggles. In the meantime, she was trying to learn how to swim. She took lessons at the college after the library closed. But she never did more than tiptoe around in the shallows. She never progressed. Her fear held her back.

When Jake started working for his father, he gave up coaching, but he never gave up the pool. He kept looking for new ones, testing them out for chlorine levels, temperatures, hours—indoors and out. He'd come back to her and report. "Melanie, I found a great pool." But, ultimately, he'd swim anywhere, wherever he could. It was that important to him.

They would spend weekends on Mission Bay, in Santa Cruz or Carmel. They had the whole California coast. They even went down to Baja. On east coast vacations they stayed on Hilton Head Island and on South Padre Island when they visited the Gulf Coast. Always there was water, water sports, and play. Melanie felt lonely most of the time. Her deceptions were beginning to wear very thin. She felt like a handicapped child, injured and afraid. She felt like she was one of the ones with polio.

When Clay moved part of his business to Asia, Jake managed the branch. Melanie and Jake lived for a month in Singapore. Melanie ran with Jake's friends through the Malaysian forests. She played cards and video games late at night with his business associates. On the weekends they'd board the rattletrap bum boats and head for the islands to snorkel. There were always more people on the boats than there were life jackets. The Malaysians had to make money. Melanie would shudder, then she'd push the dread from her mind.

It was monsoon season. They were scouting an island. The humidity could bury you. The rain came down in a curtain. Soaking wet, they took to the boat. The rain stopped as fast as it had come on. They anchored off a small cove. The boat was full of beer and snorkeling gear, and everyone—women and men—suited up and plunged over the side. They looked like neon, alien creatures bobbing about in the water. For hours they seemed to circle like that. Melanie sat and read from a book that one of the girls had given her. She drank thick, sweet Malaysian

Linda Watanabe McFerrin

coffee. Then she drank beer. The book was short, and she finished it. All around, the sea was bobbing with heads. She began to count them. She counted everyone except Jake. Every so often, a snorkeler would swim up to the boat.

"Hey, Melanie, how about a swallow of beer. Oh, great, thanks. You're a gem."

Melanie had to go to the bathroom.

"If I were in the water, I could go," she thought. "They are probably all peeing away."

Jake was the only one who hadn't swum up to the boat.

When Kenneth came by she asked, "Where's Jake?"

"Hasn't he been here?"

Melanie shook her head, "no."

"Gee, Melanie," Ken said, "I don't know. I haven't seen him." He could see something desperate in Melanie's eyes, the first gleam of panic.

His eyes quickly scanned the water's surface. "Don't worry," he counseled, "I'll try to find him." Kenneth swam off.

When Mark swam up to the boat, Melanie said, "I can't find Jake," and her voice and eyes rang with urgency. Mark said he'd tell Jake to swim back by the boat if he saw him. Melanie checked her watch. Too much time, too much time had past since she last saw him. No one knew where he was. No one was rushing to find him.

She wanted to scream his name out over the water. "Jake, Jake, where are you? Come back. I'm afraid." But she clenched her jaw and knotted her fists. She was unreasonable. He was fine. She was overreacting. Jake would be embarrassed. But how much was a reasonable amount of time? A sickness enveloped her. Her stomach was upset, and her legs were shaking. She sat frozen, counting seconds, silently begging Jake to come back to the boat.

When Jake swam up to the boat, she was angry. She tried to hide this as well. But Jake saw it in her eyes. He saw her anger, and he saw her fear.

"I'm sorry, Melanie," he said meekly.

He climbed out of the water. He wrapped his towel around her and sat next to her, holding her hand for a long time. He knew all about Melanie's brother, how he had drowned, but the tightness of her grip on his hand was startling. It made him want to cry. When everyone got back to the boat, they headed to Tioman Island, laughing and joking. Melanie didn't feel well. She and Jake went to their hut. That evening they lay on their beds, not speaking, listening to the ghostly sounds of the karaoke music wafting from the bar in the tepid island night. It got snagged and tangled in the drone of the waves as it drifted toward them.

The summer before their tenth anniversary, Jake and Melanie went to Italy. They were lucky. They stayed in a ninth century castle with five other friends. They'd selected it from a brochure filled with gleaming mansions and villas. They'd picked this one because it was only seven kilometers from the coast. They'd picked it because of the beautiful pool. The gorgeous

Tuscan sunlight cascaded down castle walls. Every day, they would lie in that sunshine, letting it bake them golden. In the mornings the housekeeper would set out the lounge chairs and drape them with fleecy blue towels. They'd read by the pool, play cards, drink chianti, and eat olives and cheese and rich pasta salads. There were rafts of various sizes stacked by the pool. Melanie sat all morning at the side of the pool, her legs dangling in the cool water. When Monica hopped in and started to goof around on a float, Melanie followed. Monica wore her sun hat in the water and all her gold jewelry. She didn't want to get her hair wet, worried that the burgundy dye would run off. Melanie paddled about in the pool. She ducked under the water and opened her eyes. Monica's chubby legs wavered before her. Melanie grabbed for them. She watched them run off to the deep end of the pool. Melanie surfaced, laughing. Monica was laughing, too, her broad lipstick grin flashing over perfect white teeth, her elbows and torso propped provocatively up on the raft.

"I'm going to catch you," Melanie said.

"I'll hide out on the deep end," Monica crooned slyly.

"You'll see," Melanie said and kicked away on her raft.

Melanie floated on her stomach and back in the shallow end of the pool—the one thing she'd learned in all of those classes.

Jake said, "Melanie, do you want me to teach you to stroke?" He got up from the card table and stood at the edge of the pool. Melanie looked at his ten swimmer's toes. She examined them closely. They made up twenty percent of his long, paddle feet.

She'd already been in the water for hours. She had started to shiver. She nodded warily.

"Okay," she said, teeth chattering, "okay, what do I do?"

Jake showed Melanie how to push through the water. He taught her to lift her elbows, relax, draw figure eights, and work less to get farther, but he wouldn't teach her to breathe.

"That's your reward when you master the stroke."

Melanie practiced the stroke every day for a week.

"Want to see me stroke?" she asked each of the friends.

"Sure, Melanie," they'd say, and they'd watch her.

Melanie swam back and forth across the width of the pool. She still couldn't breathe, but she wasn't afraid. The water wrapped around her like a cool blue gel. She felt it envelop and buoy her. It ran through her hair. It ran over her body. She could float on it, glide through it, immerse herself in it. She just couldn't swim underwater. The water would push her back up.

"See, Melanie, you're sink-proof," Jake kidded.

Melanie was surprised. She saw it was true. If she liked the water, relaxed in it, it would gather and lift her, the way Jake lifted her sometimes. These were perfect moments. The sunlight, shimmering on the water's surface, entranced her. She was hypnotized by myriad ribbons of light. She made peace with the water. She felt like a fish. She was breathtakingly happy.

It was Melanie's favorite vacation, but when she came back she wouldn't get into the water again. It was a dream, far, far away. Jake didn't push her. He'd look at her quizzically when

　　　　　　　　　　　　　　Linda Watanabe McFerrin

she'd sit by the outdoor pool at the club and watch him swim laps, her book tented over her eyes, but he said not a word. Melanie watched Jake swim back and forth in his lane—freestyle, backstroke, butterfly; butterfly was her favorite. In the lanes next to him the other swimmers kicked and crawled back and forth. Some even wore snorkels and fins. But none of them swam as quickly as Jake or had the same beautiful form.

One day when the sun was high—it must have been noon—and the lap pool was empty and quiet, Melanie picked up a kickboard and slid into the water in the lane next to Jake's. She kicked furiously, but the styrofoam board and her body angle increased the resistance.

"Kick harder," Jake said.

Melanie made it a quarter of the way down the lane. Then she buried her face in the water and kicked harder, but covered only half of the length. She was kicking like crazy, but she didn't get far.

"How's it feel?" Jake asked.

"I can't breathe," she gasped.

"Keep kicking," Jake encouraged. "You just have to practice. Your legs aren't strong enough yet."

Melanie struggled the length of the pool, then she thrashed about with her arms for a while. The lap pool was shallow. When she ran out of breath, she'd stand up. It was not like it felt at the castle. The water fought her. The lap lanes were long. Everyone else knew how to swim.

Exhausted, Melanie climbed from the pool and dried off. She sat on a chair at the pool's farthest corner and resumed her reading. Jake walked over, shaking water out of his ears.

"You okay?" he asked, sitting down next to her.

Melanie couldn't answer at first. She felt her vision grow blurry. The print in her book swam before her. She felt as if she were underwater. She was crying.

"I thought it would be easy if I loved it," she said. "It's not. I'm weak and ridiculous and I look like a geek. Does it have to be so hard?"

Jake wrapped a muscular arm around her shoulders, a big swimmer's arm, one that worked laps.

He looked down at her weepy, tear-puckered face. At that moment, she was five years old, a funny girl from Medicine Bow. She looked like the wacky kids that he taught at the pool.

"Poor Melanie," he said, laughing. "Don't worry, you'll get there."

Melanie felt his large arm tighten and lift her ever so slightly. "Not this time," she thought, and wriggled free of his embrace.

"Melanie," Jake implored, arms closing around her again. He pressed her to his chest. She felt herself drowning. She couldn't breathe. She struggled free one more time, pushing him away, pushing him hard. Melanie pursed her lips and narrowed her eyes into mean little slits.

"Jake," she said hotly, sniffling now, her fists clenched into two trembling knots, "Jake, nothing is hard for you, is it? I can't stand it anymore."

Linda Watanabe McFerrin

"What do you mean?" Jake asked warily. He'd never seen Melanie like this before, her face scrunched and angry. She was furious.

"Jake," she said fiercely. "Nothing. Nothing phases you, does it?"

Jake sensed somehow that this was a monumental issue. One that he could not address with the buoyancy with which he handled everything else in his life.

"You're wrong, Melanie," he said simply. "Water scares you. Sometimes you scare me. You are unfathomable. There all these hidden currents with you. I never know what to expect. But I don't give up. You're too important to me."

Melanie looked up at Jake, at the startled blink-blink of his eyes, the way they clouded and cleared. That's all she saw because at that moment the dam broke; the frustration of years poured through the floodgates. Relief rolled over her. She shut her eyes tightly and let herself be carried away by the seas that continually swirled around them, the sea of Jake's laughter, the sea of her tears.

A Little Variety

"What this country is losing, what is going the way of the dinosaur, is the good old-fashioned variety store—the five-and-dime," thought Mona as she pushed her gardening hat down over her fluffy gray hair and charged down the hill into the hustle and bustle of her Sunset District neighborhood. Living in San Francisco, with the world virtually at her doorstep, Mona rarely found an occasion to go more than a few blocks to find anything. Wal-Mart and Kmart might be part of the nineties, but they couldn't replace the variety store of her youth. Her neighborhood had one of the last of them.

All her life Mona had found everything she had ever wanted or needed at the variety store, Harvey's Variety Five and Dime, to be exact—including her husband Ed. She smiled when she thought of Ed. Now *he* was a real find. What had she gone in for that day? Several packets of seeds—marigolds, dahlias, bachelor buttons—the kind of flowers that are colorful. Loud, friendly flowers. Not the airy-fairy, fancy-dancy kind. Mona liked flowers that could cheer people up. Snapdragons, daisies— she had plenty of those, too.

On that particular day, April 3, 1992, she had stopped first to have lunch—a burger at Jake's. Jake's Diner, Millie's Thrift, Gallagher's Stationery, Bill's Gaslight, Clausen's Market—almost every business on Irving street had someone's name connected with it, and the owners—Jake, Harvey, Millie, Bill, Ella Gallagher, and Harold Clausen—were always in their shops, working away. Mona knew them all, too, at least on a speaking-to basis. She chatted with most of them daily. In fact, she chatted with just about everyone she encountered on Irving Street—students, housewives, strangers—the kind of people who were out and about during the day. Sometimes, she'd sit across from the five-and-dime and watch them come and go—on foot, on bikes, in their run-down, can-no-longer-open-the-window cars. Once she had been entertained for a full thirty minutes watching a kid break into his own car because the door was jammed.

Harvey's Variety Five and Dime, on the opposite side of the street from Jake's Diner, was wedged between Millie's Thrift shop and Gallagher's Stationery. Mona did a lot of business at both. "Yep," Mona smiled, thinking about the pretty blue paper at Gallagher's. She had time to write letters. People like her had that kind of time, spent the latter part of their lives giving away the things they'd gathered around them in the first half. In fact it was on people like Mona that people like Millie thrived; and by the look of Millie's, crammed to the jambs with merchandise, there were plenty of people like Mona—people with cheap, quirky taste.

"But you know," Mona thought, "even *that* gets better with

Linda Watanabe McFerrin

age." In fact, Mona's tastes represented just what everyone seemed to be looking for. Like the college students who shopped at the thrift store; they were Millie's best customers. They were in love with tacky old things. They seemed to be drawn to them, as if there were something secretly magical about carnival glass and homemade ceramics.

Mona always made it a point to eavesdrop on their conversations. It was like listening to someone talking about you behind your back. They said things like:

"Oh, Jen, look at this. Can you believe it? My mother had one of these."

"Oh my, isn't it just too trashy; and look at that silly fringe. Look, if you don't get it, I will. How much is it?"

"$3.50."

"$3.50? God, I can't believe it. This place is so fabulous. They don't even know what they have. Scoop it up."

"A bargain."

"Oh, yeah, a bargain." Mona snorted. "One man's garbage . . . Yeah, life is a bargain." Those cute, sassy kids in their crazy put-together clothes, talking about the fifties as if they were prehistoric—she loved them. They were making her life worthwhile.

The streetcar rattled by—the "N" Judah car. Mona wondered how long it would be before they replaced the remaining electric cars with greasy fume-spewing buses.

"Just a matter of time," she thought. "Hang on," she muttered addressing the streetcar, "hang on."

A few buildings up, across the street, was the old lounge, Bill's Gaslight. Fire escapes dangled from the apartment windows above it, a clutter of ugly balconies.

"Fire escapes," Mona reflected, "are like radiators—unattractive, but ultimately useful." You had to wait until they wore out to replace them, and that seemed to take a very long time. Like her. She was not wearing out, not at all.

Eating her hamburger on that momentous day, two years ago, Mona was pleased. From her window seat at Jake's Grill she had a good view of Harvey's. If anything exciting happened, she could pounce. Mona hated to miss things. And she didn't. She never missed a sale, never missed a bargain.

Harvey's Variety was having a sale, a special on seeds, and Mona planned to stock up. But she wanted to savor the feeling, wanted to take it slow, wanted to kind of sneak up on it. She wanted to get the most bang for her buck, and she loved the anticipation. So she decided to wait. She decided to have lunch at Jake's and wait till the spirit moved her.

Just to the left of the store, out on the sidewalk, Harvey had arranged several trash cans. They bristled with the long handles of various mops and brooms.

"Spring cleaning," mused Mona, imagining herself with a kerchief tied around her head. It was funny. Young girls wore their hair that way all the time. She'd seen them at Millie's, spongy pink dish towels tied around their cropped hair, again validating her life. She straightened her shoulders. Things like that made her feel important. Spring cleaning was Mona's favorite spring ritual, more significant than a month of Easters and Ash Wednesdays.

She was thinking just that. She was also thinking about the seeds, yes, but at the top of her mind was the phrase, "spring cleaning." "SPRING CLEANING"—she could almost see it in front of her now, like a big, neon sign. She was musing like that when a handsome young man in a white T-shirt and shorts walked almost past Harvey's and stopped. How odd. He was hauling a huge Hefty trash bag full of clothes. He was dragging it along the sidewalk behind him. The bag was ripping on the concrete walk and clothes were dribbling from it. He kept stopping to pick up the clothes that fell out, stuffing them under his arm. As the bag became emptier and emptier, the knot of clothing under his arm got bigger and bigger until it was almost impossible to manage. But the part that Mona loved remembering the most was that in the midst of all this, he stopped. He stopped as he passed the variety store. He stopped right in front of the trash cans with all the mops and the brooms in them, and Mona could see it—in his head, too—like a neon sign, those words: "SPRING CLEANING." It really was such an uplifting phrase. Mona thought she saw him relax for a moment. He straightened, then, from dragging his bag, and stretched, and she saw that he must be around six-foot-two-inches, and he had broad shoulders. Well, Mona was out of her seat and across the street in a snap, because she knew an opportunity when she saw one.

She rushed over to Harvey's door and, whoops, she "accidentally" bumped right into the young man, wham, as she tried to rush past him. He looked down at her, somewhat surprised, having no idea where she'd come from. Mona knew that he was sizing her up. And she knew that she was quite a sight in her yellow capri pants, her gardening hat, her plastic fruit-covered sandals, and the cotton front of her bowling-style shirt waterfalling over her D-cup breasts. "One thing never goes out of style," she thought with a world-wise chuckle. It looked like all six-foot-two-inches of him was going to reel backward, caught up as he was in the middle of private thoughts.

"Young man," Mona said with just the right touch of kindness and humor, indicating the clothes under his arm and the near-empty bag at his feet, "what you need is a shopping cart."

Suddenly he was aware of himself, gently weaned from the image of Mona's goofy hat, the plastic fruit-covered sandals, and the D-cup breasts. He realized that he must also look somewhat ridiculous with the trash bag pooling around his feet and his underarms stuffed full of clothes.

"Laundry?" Mona asked charitably.

"Oh, no, not exactly," he answered, still off guard and feeling a little silly. "I was just thinking," he said confessionally, nodding toward the cans full of mops and brooms, "I was just thinking about spring cleaning."

There they were again. Those magic words. They meant marvelous things to Mona—like sales, bargains, longer days,

Linda Watanabe McFerrin

summer, fresh starts, and six-foot-two-inch guys with their arms full of laundry.

"Oh," she laughed, "and I was running into Harvey's for seeds. You know," she said, patting the top of her hat theatrically, "it's planting time." Mona delivered this with just the right touch of hayseed—a cross between Ethel Merman and Minnie Pearl. She knew how to work her era, knew how to capitalize on that undiminishable source of charm.

"Need any help?" she asked in her most neighborly way.

The young man looked down at her again, running a big hand through his longish sun-streaked hair. Mona liked that he was wearing a kind of bracelet and that his T-shirt had the words, "NOT BAD/NOT RAD," on it. She also liked the sweaty smell that floated around him. She wasn't around that kind of smell much anymore.

The young man looked at her as if she had made a truly bizarre proposition. He had dropped a few T-shirts unnoticed, when he ran his hand through his hair again. He gazed down at them suddenly conscious of this. "Well, yeah, I guess I could use a little help," he said warily. "I'm just going a few doors up—to Millie's."

Mona smiled a broad, watermelon-red smile. "To Millie's," she said, delightedly stooping to pick up a few sweat-scented T-shirts. "Well, come on then. By the way," she added sweetly, "my name's Mona. And you?"

"Me? Oh, yes, sorry. My name's Ed."

Millie Salinger pursed her lips and squinted when Ed and Mona walked in the door. She fished around in the drawer and pulled out a pair of cat's-eye bifocals. They certainly were an unlikely couple, but Millie was having one of her "feelings." It was as if she had seen them together before.

"Hey, Millie," Ed greeted the thrift-store proprietor.

"Just put your things here in this box, honey," Millie said sweetly. "Well, Mona," she added, addressing her longtime friend. They'd gone to high school and business college together. "Whatever are you up to?"

Ed dumped the dirty garments into the box, then made his way through the clothing-crammed interior of the shop, finding and focusing on one rack of T-shirts and another of pants.

"He comes here every week," Millie whispered to Mona with a nod in Ed's direction. "He brings in his soiled clothing and buys things to replace them. Perfectly sweet guy," she added, as if he were in some way handicapped. "Just can't do laundry. Look at this," she said, pulling a pair of gaudy, green paisley boxer shorts out of the box on the counter. "I have to wash everything. It's like taking in laundry."

"You trade his dirty clothes for new ones?" Mona asked with concern. It wasn't like Millie to get stuck with the short end of a deal.

"Of course not, silly," Millie said with a wink. "I just use the old stuff to discount his purchase. It's a kind of recycling, a deposit system, like used Coke bottles or something." Mona was glad to hear that Millie and Ed had only business between them.

"He's cute, don't you think?" Millie asked, knowing Mona well enough to have sensed the attraction.

Linda Watanabe McFerrin

Mona laughed. "He's a doll."

"And young," Millie added, pressing a point. "Twenty-seven years old. Saw it on his driver's license."

Mona looked at her friend and sighed audibly. "Millie," she said, "we mustn't hold that against him."

Ed came back to the counter with an armload of T-shirts, three pairs of shorts, and some slacks. "These, Millie," he announced with a wide, winning grin.

Millie counted the shirts and folded the pants. "That's $15.95 for the lot, Ed," she said. "I give him a bit of a discount," she confided loudly to Mona.

Ed paid the $15.95. "Thank you, Millie," he said. "You're a gem."

"See you next week," Millie sang as she rang up the sale.

"So, Ed," Mona asked when they walked out the door. "So, you never do laundry?"

"No, I don't," Ed replied sheepishly. "I have fabric care problems. Things shrink and change color. It's much easier this way. Millie takes care of everything. And thanks, by the way, for your help," he added with feeling. "I'd like to reciprocate. If you're here to get seeds I can help you with that. I'm an awesome gardener, you know."

So they went back to Harvey's Variety Five and Dime, and in addition to dahlias and bachelor buttons, Mona bought sweet peas that day. She bought zinnias, pansies, and carnations. She bought corn, tomatoes, zucchini, and eggplant. She bought lettuce and carrots and baby potatoes.

Ed carried everything up the hill to her house. He offered to help plant the garden.

All summer long he watered and hoed in the big plot in Mona's backyard. Mona made zucchini fritatas and tomato salsas. She taught Ed how to do laundry. She made eggplant ragouts and potato pancakes. And when summer had passed and the garden died back, Ed moved in with Mona.

"Next year," Ed said, one evening in December, as he folded fluffy, clean towels, "we'll plant bush beans and jasmine. Wouldn't you love to cover that fence with climbers and flowers?"

"Yes," said Mona, "that's a good idea, Ed." She'd lived with bare chain-link for years. A change would be welcome. "Or we could take the fence down," she offered.

"No, Mona," Ed said thoughtfully. He paused in his folding. "The fence is still strong. We don't need to replace it."

So they covered the fence with bush beans and jasmine, and when fall came again, they were married between it and the garden.

Millie came to the wedding. So did Bill and Jake and Mr. and Mrs. Clausen. Harvey also made an appearance.

Harvey said, "Mona, I don't know what to give you. You can take your pick from anything there in the store. Just take it."

Mona laughed out loud. She'd found the best gift of all right on his threshold.

"Oh, I don't know, Harvey," she said, "you have so many things. Why don't you just surprise me?"

God and All the Angels

When Terrell's mama, Maiva, died, Selita went to the funeral. She sat tall in the twelfth row of the 96th Avenue Baptist Church, as composed as a television anchor woman, while everyone else carried on.

She had liked Terrell's mama, and Terrell's mama had liked her; so she was glad to be paying her respects. Of course, no one knew that for Maiva, who had crossed over into another world, Selita was the most important person in the room. To the throng that sweated, fidgeted, swayed, and soared to spiritual heights on the wake of Maiva's heavenly transportation, Selita was no more than another of Terrell's many girlfriends. The most recent one perhaps, but beyond that, nothing special. She wasn't the most ingratiating, or the prettiest, or the most enamored with Terrell. And she certainly wasn't the only girlfriend in attendance. The knife-and-scissors-scored pews of that shabby little church were generously salted with the lovers of Maiva's cherished only son.

With the exception of Selita, none of Terrell's girlfriends were very much interested in either the personality or the metaphysical destiny of his mama, Maiva Quinn. Most of them didn't even like her. And she hadn't liked them. Like a closetful of cheap nylon nightgowns, they seemed only marginally alluring and infinitely replaceable. They had come to the funeral, not for Maiva, but for Terrell and for the chance to catwalk solicitously back into his consciousness. But for the time being, focused as he was on his mother's casket, Terrell took no notice of them.

The most important woman in Terrell's life was dead, and he felt really bad. The fact that every available seat was taken and that the room was swollen with family members, neighbors, Maiva's choir and church and card and gardening friends, and so many of the other women in his life made very little difference to him. He didn't notice, either, how the light trumpeted in that Sunday morning in July through the six frosted panes that towered over the front door of the church to settle, like a shine on ebony, over the gentle rise of Maiva's brow and cheekbones, or how it pummeled the star-and-trapezoid-shaped holes in the walls where loose plaster had fallen to reveal the rotting ribwork of lath. The church was gay with the flowers of Maiva's gardening buddies, many of whom had risen to testify to her great character and strength, but Terrell, self-absorbed and utterly miserable, barely noted that.

Maiva, on the other hand, had she been in the body, would have loved the flowers. She would have deeply inhaled the scent of lilies, lilacs, gardenias, and floribunda roses. Her heart would have sprouted sudden tendrils of tenderness at the flatteries of

Linda Watanabe McFerrin

her friends. And she would have clapped, nodded, and "amened" to the Reverend John Wort's sermon about the fact that she, Maiva Quinn, was *expected* in the Kingdom of the Lord. That there was a place set for her at the table of *Jesus*. That her recipe for life would be *welcome* at God's banquet. Maiva would also have loved the way her nasty sister, Cora Mae, threw herself on the coffin to make her big-skirted, stiff-hatted, sorrowful amends because she and Maiva had been fighting for so many years, and like any big winner, Cora Mae could afford to put on a show. And she would have especially loved that her precious boy, Terrell, was sitting just a few feet away from her, already missing her terribly, and that his current girlfriend, Selita, was seated, considerately, somewhere toward the middle of the church paying her respects. Selita was a capable and dependable young woman. That made her quite unlike the flighty creatures with whom Terrell ordinarily consorted. And that made Selita special.

In addition to the quick sensual survey and a certain satisfaction with Selita's attendance and other ceremonial details, Maiva's attention—had she been physically present—would have been focused also on another feminine entity, this one six years old and wriggling on the seat next to her daddy. This pint-sized being was Terrell's daughter, Tina, and Maiva's only grandchild. Something that would have certainly irritated Maiva— the same thing that disturbed both Terrell and Selita—was that Aisha, Tina's mother, was also seated in the front row, clinging possessively to Tina, flaunting her hold on Terrell, and making everyone's life a horror. Maiva would have sympathized deeply with Tina, who squirmed away from Aisha and tried to snuggle closer to a father who paid her no attention. Even at six, Tina was aware that she was no more than a pawn. Her mama always made a big fuss over her in front of people and when they were alone, ignored her. This was very different from the care she had received from her grandmother, who spoiled her both in public and in private; from Terrell, who was not even remotely interested in her; and from the care she was about to receive from Selita, who was to prove as perpetual and immutable as the road between her house and her school.

In her struggle to move closer to her father, Tina accidentally pinched the inside of his thigh with a knobby little elbow, waking him from his sullen reverie. Terrell looked at the thin-limbed, pixie copy of manipulative Aisha and turned to find Selita's face in the sea that swam behind him. She, he thought, could save him from the baby mama who dangled Tina like a baited hook in front of him at every opportunity.

Perhaps it was the counterinfluence of Terrell's indifference and Aisha's shammed devotion that prompted Tina to slide from the pew, highstep up to the casket, and wrestle a place for herself right next to Cora Mae's queen-sized posterior. The casket, which had been purchased from Alex Buniole's Funeral Heaven, was as black as pitch. It had big, gold-plated handles and a lining of fuchsia satin that Tina could just see peeking out at her from the coffin's top. Tina, who could not see over the side

Linda Watanabe McFerrin

of the well-polished sarcophagus even though she got up on her tiptoes, was not convinced that her grandmother was really in the dark, rectangular box at all. If she were, Tina decided, she'd be submerged—half-drowned in the crocodile tears that Cora Mae was raining liberally into it. Imagining a swimming pool with her grandmother floating upon it on an inflatable raft, a glass of pink lemonade bobbing next to her like a camellia decorating a punch bowl, Tina offered up a prayer.

The prayer is untranslatable because Tina could not cast the vague shape of her longing into language. But for Maiva, and anyone dwelling in the astral world for that matter, the wish came in clear as a bell. Formless beings prefer formless thoughts. Dead people have trouble with language.

If Maiva had not already stepped across the boundary to the other side, she would have sat up in her coffin, pushed the theatrical Cora Mae out of the way, and wrapped her arms around Tina. As it was, all she could do was send out a comforting vibe so that when Tina finished her prayer and opened her downcast eyes, the white ruffle of her anklet socks looked as frothy as angel wings and the shine in her black mary janes beamed up at her like a kiss. It was this luster that walked with her back to the pew where a much-comforted Tina resumed her place in the fractious embrace of her family.

After the tributes and the sermon, the choir raised its voice in praise of the Lord, and it was this song that carried Maiva finally up the celestial staircase. More plaster must have fallen during that outburst of affection and celebration, star metamorphosing into trapezoid, trapezoid into rhombus on the dusty old walls of church. When the funeral was over, the congregation stepped outside into the 96th Avenue sunshine. Under a canopy of a baby-blue sky dotted with clouds shaped like wispy rosettes, the family and friends of Maiva Quinn touched, knitted, and knotted, embroidering the morning with rich combinations of jubilation and warmth. Aisha stood as close to Terrell as she possibly could, her arms wound tightly around Tina, Terrell disregarding their proximity as the procession of young women with whom he had dallied came up to express their regrets.

In a dizzying parade of scent, short skirts, high-heeled shoes, sculpted nails, and elaborate hairdos, Terrell's ladies sauntered up to offer their silky condolences to Maiva's bereaved boy. Aisha, struggling against this upwelling of her ex-boyfriend's old loves, kept her violet-colored talons firmly planted in the only piece of Terrell's flesh to which she could still lay claim—a much bigger piece, she surmised, than anything those other women did possess. Selita, looking elegant and aloof in her orchid-colored suit, leaned up against her car, a silver Lexus that she'd parked wisely and portentously right in front of the church like a coachman with the perfect exit strategy. The car keys dangling from her manicured fingertips flashed like an approach light on a runway, and Terrell, gratefully honing in on them, made his excuses, untangled himself from the garrote of past encounters, and with a relief that was clear and visible said, "Save me, Selita. Let's get out of here."

Selita nodded, opened the door for him, and let herself in on the driver's side.

"Where to?" she asked.

"Let's go to the club," Terrell replied, thinking that a Remy was exactly what he needed in the misty-eyed middle of that morning.

Selita glanced over at Terrell, considering for a moment his handsome face and build, how fine he looked all suited up, the tight curl of his hair. "Lots of girlfriends," she observed coolly, her full lips anticipatory, just a little open, as if poised for a pronouncement.

Terrell, conflicted as always between the good his mama saw in Selita and her physical attractiveness, looked at her and sighed. "Uh, huh," he agreed, straightening a sleeve.

It didn't take Aisha long to project her desires into the vacuum left in Maiva's absence. With Terrell's main gatekeeper gone, she stormed at once the citadel of his attentions. She called him up the very evening of Maiva's funeral to demand that he take care of Tina while she "went to get her club on" with her friends. Tina was, as usual, the genetic hostage through whom she could exact a ransom.

Of course Terrell said no. She always called him without notice. He had made other plans. Besides, his mama had just died. What was Aisha trying to do? His voice rose on the phone. Aisha's voice rose with it.

"You, Terrell, have never been a father to this child. How come you don't care about Tina, huh? She's your baby, too.

You're never there for her. It's all about you, isn't it, Terrell? You and those trifling hos you hang out with. Maiva may be dead, but you are still nothing but a mama's boy. You just don't have that big skirt to hide behind anymore now that she's gone."

Tina, her hand caught fast in Aisha's angry grip, could not squirm free to cover her ears the way she wanted to—she hated it when her mama talked this way—so she let out a squeal.

"Is Tina there?" Terrell asked angrily.

"'Course she is," Aisha taunted. "You think I hide the truth from her? Cover up for your behavior?"

"All right, all right," Terrell's voice placated. "I'll come and get her." Then he slammed down the phone.

He quickly dialed Selita's number.

Terrell despised the way Aisha used Tina to make him do things for her. The truth was he could have loved his daughter, but with every step he made toward her Aisha tightened the noose around his neck. Tina was the trap that Aisha had set for Terrell seven years ago when they were dating. Her plan had failed. She had not managed to catch Terrell, but she had found a way to keep him on an emotional tether. Maiva's love for Tina, Terrell's potential love for Tina—all this kept him bound to her financially and otherwise. Terrell supported Tina, Aisha by association, and physically he tried to keep his distance. But Aisha knew just how strong the tie was between the father and his child, and when he got too free, too spirited, she'd pull him in.

"Hello?" Selita's voice sounded sleepy on the phone.

Linda Watanabe McFerrin

"Baby, did I wake you?"

"Um, hmm. What time is it? Oh, I must have fallen asleep. Terrell, I simply cannot drink a whiskey in the middle of the day. How are you doing, honey?"

"Me? Oh, I'm straight. It's just that Aisha called me to watch Tina tonight, and I can't. So, Selita, I was wondering if . . ."

It was so easy for Terrell to slip the yoke, to transfer the responsibility that Maiva had assumed for him to Selita. She was so much like Maiva anyway—caring, thoughtful, and dependable. She was the only woman Terrell had dealings with who had a career. Perhaps that was why the two women had been so drawn to one another. For Terrell, these very qualities presented problems. The only thing that made it possible for him to love Selita at all was her beauty. In this way, she was not a bit like Maiva, at least not to Terrell. In his mind Selita was far lovelier than any of his other girlfriends. Of course, it did not occur to him that this loveliness had to do with something more than physical appearance. That would have disturbed Terrell. He liked to think his preference for Selita had to do with her prettiness.

"You want me to take care of Tina for you?" Selita said warily. She was a little cat shy after witnessing the pussy promenade at the funeral and not enthusiastic about getting any closer to Aisha.

"Just this once, sweetie," Terrell pleaded. "It's been a hard day. I just can't do it tonight."

"All right, Terrell," Selita heard herself say, regretting almost immediately her acquiescence. "You'll drop her off, right?"

"Yes. Oh, thank you, baby. I'll make it up to you. You know how much this means to me."

"Ummm," said Selita, shaking her whiskey head. She hung up with Terrell and took a shower.

Tina sat quietly in the car next to Terrell. She knew he was taking her to one of his girlfriends for the evening. In the past his surrogate had always been Maiva. But as Terrell had so crisply clarified, Grandma was gone now. Tina would spend the evening with Selita.

"Mama's gonna be mad if she finds out you took me to your girlfriend's house," Tina muttered.

"You are too young to be in my adult business. Maybe we just won't tell her," said Terrell.

"Maybe. What will you give me if I keep the secret?"

"Girl, where did you learn that blackmail shit? Don't tell me. From your mama. Six years old and you're already trying that blackmail shit on me."

Terrell took the next corner tightly. The car screeched angrily beneath them. Tina knew she'd made him really mad. It scared her, so she wasn't going to say another word.

"You just better be a good girl with Selita," warned Terrell. "I don't want to hear about any misbehavior. And I don't want you talking with your mama's mouth. Look where it gets her—a whole lot of nowhere. Nobody's gonna want to be around you if you act like her."

The problem was that Tina didn't really know how else to act.

Linda Watanabe McFerrin

One thing Tina didn't have to do was feign surprise when they arrived at Selita's place. It was across town, near a lake that twinkled in a necklace of lights slung from light pole to light pole around it. The building looked like a beautiful box wrapped in gray paper and trimmed in fancy white ribbon. It had a wide, marble-floored lobby and an elevator that took Tina and her daddy up to the seventh floor. Selita came to the door, kissed Terrell quickly on the cheek, and then smiled down at Tina. She was wearing a freshly laundered white shirt and a pair of black sweatpants. Her feet were bare, and she had gold nail polish on her toenails.

"Well, hi there, Tina," said Selita.

Tina said nothing, stuck her little nose up in the air, and swaggered in.

Selita followed, closing the door on Terrell who had kissed her, gushed bouquets of thank yous, and hurried back toward the elevator.

"I've been on that lake," Tina lied before she had removed her coat. "In a big boat. With my mama."

"Really?" said Selita, already certain that it was going to be a long and trying evening.

"Yes. And we have a big house, too. With lots of things in it. It's not empty like this." What Tina didn't want to say was that she lived in a tiny apartment that was always messy. She saw immediately that Selita's home was neat and so sparsely furnished that everything in it seemed very, very special. The walls were lavender, the ceiling was light green, and most of the furniture was white except for one purple velvet chair that Tina was dying to sit in. The dining room table had been set with napkins, plates, and silverware, and there were candles on it.

"You haven't had dinner yet, have you?" asked Selita, noting the direction of Tina's gaze.

"No. I like McDonald's," Tina said meaningfully. "That's what we always have."

"Well, I don't have that, but I can give you chicken soup and a great big bowl of cut-up fruit—bananas, strawberries, kiwi, pineapple—how does that sound? Oh, I almost forgot—and chocolate cake for dessert."

Tina shrugged. She didn't know what kiwi was, but she liked the sound of the fruit, and of course she wanted chocolate cake. "I'd rather have McDonald's," she complained.

Selita ignored this. In minutes she had the food set on the table.

"If you used plastic forks and plates you wouldn't have to clean this up," said Tina critically as she swung her legs beneath her during dinner. She liked the shiny gold and purple design on Selita's dishes, imagined how they'd look piled up on top of one another on the kitchen counter. "And paper napkins are better, too, because you throw them away. My mama's beautiful, and she's got lots of boyfriends," she added suddenly.

Selita looked a little startled. "Your mama's very pretty," she agreed.

Tina thought that Selita was also very beautiful, but she didn't like her. She didn't like Selita, and she didn't like her too-

Linda Watanabe McFerrin

clean, fancy house. "I want to watch a movie now," she said.

Selita seated Tina in the purple velvet chair to watch the movie. Tina fell asleep there, curled up in its soft, plush lap. That's where Terrell found her when he came to pick her up.

What Terrell didn't tell Selita was that he couldn't watch Tina that evening because he had a date. Lavonne was such a nasty girl. Terrell had forgotten how good bad girls could be, but she had reminded him very quickly at the funeral. A touch here, a tongue there, when she hugged him and put her phone number in his pocket. What with the terrible stress of his mother dying, he thought the booty call would be just the thing to perk him up. And he was right. What he hadn't counted on was just how addicting a woman like Lavonne could be. He'd gone out with her briefly a few years before, and he'd dropped her—he'd forgotten why. It seemed she'd been around a lot since then; her talents had developed. She was a big girl, too, and quite demanding, the kind that kept a man's hands full in every possible way. Selita's attributes paled next to Lavonne's big-breasted, thick-thighed urgings.

Of course Terrell said nothing of this to Selita. There was Maiva's role to fill for Tina, and Selita seemed the perfect candidate for the job. Perhaps, had Maiva been alive, she would have been appalled by what Terrell was doing. But after all, she knew her son. She'd never interfered with his love life, however sticky things managed to get between him and the objects of his fickle affections. More likely Maiva would have been greatly pleased and far more interested in what was going on between her granddaughter and her son's soon-to-be-ex-girlfriend. Selita was really much too good for Terrell.

It pained Selita, naturally, that Tina lied and copped an attitude that could easily make one want to avoid her. But there was something about the little girl that touched her heart. Tina reminded her, in the tiniest way, of Maiva. Some of her grandma's frank and forceful nature had rubbed off on the child. But what Selita didn't know was that she had actually been captured by Tina's wordless prayer. Tina had sent out a call for help, one that Selita had been chosen to answer. All that Selita knew was that something about the sweet-faced imp of a girl snoring away in the purple chair spoke to her, and this is what prompted her to pay Tina's great-aunt, Cora Mae, a visit.

It was apparent to just about everyone who had known Maiva and Cora Mae that the sisters were absolute opposites. Maiva loved flowers and music and people, and especially Terrell and Tina, while Cora Mae loved money and what it could buy. She liked food, big hats, and loads of expensive shoes. She did not trust anyone, least of all her family; she thought Terrell was a philanderer and that her grandniece, Tina, was a brat. She did have one thing in common with her dead sister, however. She liked Selita a lot. So when the young woman called her with things on her mind, she was pleased to invite her to tea.

Cora Mae lived in great style in a house in the hills with two surly Dobermans and a big swimming pool. It was this pool that

Linda Watanabe McFerrin

had inspired Tina's coffin-side vision, and it was next to this pool that Cora Mae served her tea.

"Actually, I came to you to talk about Tina," Selita revealed once they'd settled into their teacups.

"Just like her mama and papa," spat Cora Mae. "Ugh, that child is a demon."

"I know it seems that way, but I think it's an act. She has no place to turn, Cora Mae. I went to pick her up at school the other day—Aisha couldn't do it, and Terrell was tied up, so he asked me if I'd fetch her and take her home. Well, when I drove up, Tina was standing in the middle of the playground, and a long line of girls was hurling insults at her. Liar. Stinky. Baby bitch. Their taunts were awful. Tina stood her ground even when one of her tormentors, a very big girl, ran up and pushed her. A teacher came out and broke it all up before I could park and get out of the car. Tina seemed glad to see me. She didn't ask about Aisha or about Terrell, and she didn't know that I'd seen the abuse that she'd taken. On the way home she told me all about how popular she was at school and how all her friends wished that their mamas were as pretty as hers.

"When we got to the apartment, there was no one at home, so we waited in the car—two hours, Cora Mae, until Aisha arrived. All Aisha could do was swear on Terrell. She was furious with him, furious with me, furious even with Tina. I was just wondering . . . you've known them for such a long time, is there anything I can do to help Tina?"

Cora Mae was taken completely off guard by Selita's account and by her request for advice. Normally, she would have snorted a perfunctory "don't think so" and called it a visit. But she had been standing next to Tina at the funeral when the child offered up her unphraseable prayer. The petition had grazed her as it launched heavenward, and like Selita, she had been caught in its potency.

"I don't know," she admitted with a sigh that suited her girth. "Some things are unsalvageable, like the rift between Maiva and me. Nothing this side of heaven could make us see eye to eye. But I know what you mean. That little girl is a mess. She's just like her mama. Unwanted. Unloved. And she's acting it out every hour, every minute. Can anyone get through to that Tina? I don't think so. It will take God and all the angels to save that child."

Cora Mae felt suddenly heavy in her heart and her soul. She just wanted to cry. "I'm sorry, Selita, I don't think I can help you. I wish I could, but I can't." She pushed back her chair and gathered the dirty teacups. Tina's prayer shot into the galaxy on giant booster rockets and started to unfurl like a banner.

Aisha could see the bond that was forming between Tina and Selita. It troubled her in a strange and upsetting way. Some stammering part of her mind seemed to deem it a very good thing—for Tina, but not for her. She could no longer blackmail Terrell with Tina's emotional needs. She called Terrell, Terrell called Selita, and Selita no longer seemed to be just filling in. Selita clearly enjoyed spending time with Tina, even though Tina responded with no particular show of affection. Even so,

Linda Watanabe McFerrin

this attention to Tina made Aisha terribly jealous. She began to compete with Selita, finding, of course, that she herself had a much greater hold on her daughter's heart than she had ever imagined. This lovely discovery should have been enough for Aisha, but she was so consumed by her need to control Terrell and curtail any freedom that he might be able to contrive that she began looking about for some poison.

She found it in Terrell's ongoing fling with Lavonne—Aisha had lots of connections in the same scene as Terrell—and she made it a point to pen the note that would so inform Selita. Late one night, with a profound and satisfied chuckle, she dropped her letter into the mail slot at Selita's apartment. There was no way she'd trust the mail with the mission.

Selita was a little surprised by the crude language of Aisha's missive, but she wasn't exactly staggered by its content. She suspected Terrell of affairs; she knew his past, but she'd been so absorbed with her growing affection for Tina that she'd all but shut his methods of operation from her mind. For a moment she actually considered pretending she hadn't received the letter, worried about what it would do to the support that she was trying to give to Tina. She realized, however, that since it had been written by Aisha, to ignore it would be impossible. Selita called Terrell, told him what she'd discovered, and let him know that it was over for them. All Terrell had to say was, "What about Tina?"

Selita knew she had to tell Tina about breaking up with Terrell. Very likely she wouldn't be baby sitting anymore or picking Tina up from school. This was not something she wanted to do at Aisha's apartment, so she went to Tina's school, waiting outside the chain-link-fenced schoolyard. Children exploded out of the doors at recess, Tina among them. She seemed to have made a friend. The two little girls looked over at Selita where she waved from the other side of the barrier. Tina said something to her new playmate who sat down on the steps while Tina walked up to Selita.

"Why are you here?" said Tina accusingly, as if embarrassed by Selita's presence.

"Well, I just want to tell you that I'm no longer your daddy's girlfriend. I've just been advised that he's seeing someone else."

"So?" mumbled Tina testily.

"So, I'm breaking up with him."

"Just because of another woman? That's how he is."

"Yes, it is, and that's why I can't stay with him."

"But what will you do?" Tina sharply inquired.

"Oh, don't worry about me," Selita laughed. "I'll get along fine without him."

"You'd leave him just like that?"

"You have to, honey, when it just isn't right." Selita had crouched down to talk to Tina. She stood and smiled sadly. "I just wanted you to know," she concluded.

"You're going to leave me, too?" Tina accused. She thrust her thin hands and skinny arms out through the chain-link of the fence. Selita looked down at the little fist of a face clenched with Tina's disappointment.

"Of course not, Tina," she said slowly and gravely. "I'm just leaving Terrell. I'll always be there for you." She took Tina's hands and cupped them between hers—one prayer locked tightly within another. Maiva put her arms around both of them even though she was no longer in the body, and overhead Tina's big purple banner unfurled. "I love you, Tina," it said.

Pickled Eggs

It was 10:05 P.M. on Giselle's biological clock with no husband in sight. She wasn't exactly sure when egg production would stop. Her mother had died when Giselle was thirty and had taken the secret with her. Giselle was sure, however, that the cataclysmic change was just around the corner, and she was worried.

This was a new worry, one that squeezed comfortably in to join the family of similar squatters that over the years had taken up residence in her mind. She'd been collecting them since she had her first vague presentiment that there was something more than the continuous present. Her very first worry, she seemed to recall, had something to do with her mother leaving the room. Giselle, reclining innocently in her little white crib, suddenly overwhelmed with the fear that the only person she could count on was not coming back, had scrunched up her face and cried. Oddly, this worry never did go away. It persisted until her mother, who had cancer, really did disappear for good. That was the history of Giselle's earliest worry and its outcome. Worries, ignored, become premonitions. Giselle knew that for certain.

As the years progressed and Giselle's world expanded, other worries came to join hands with the first. The fear that other kids in the school wouldn't like her—she was, after all, always a new kid, a career diplomat's daughter with the out-of-place manners of whatever out-of-the-way place that her father had last been assigned. The fear that she wouldn't be asked to dance—she was taller than most of the boys and too thin. The fear that someone would actually call some of the numbers she'd put on her resume—she felt her experience should at least fill the page. The fear that Prince Charming would arrive after menopause and that Cinderella would be short a lot more than one slipper.

Most of her worries matured rather uncomfortably into facts, and Giselle was worried that this latest worry, left unattended, was destined to do the same.

"So, what do you know about egg harvesting?" she asked her dear friend, Elena, as they sipped at a pair of watery Cape Cods in the bar at the La Cambodienne.

"Like free-range or incubated?" Elena asked looking up from the thin red straw she was twirling around in the cranberry-colored liquid. Cranberry juice, they both knew, was good for the bladder.

"No, like models selling theirs to the highest bidder. That kind of thing," corrected Giselle. "I'm thinking about getting it done."

"Hey, super idea." Elena looked delighted. "How much do you think you could get?"

Giselle laughed, flattered that Elena had so easily assumed and accepted that she could even imagine marketing herself in

Linda Watanabe McFerrin

that way. "No, I don't mean that I want to sell them. It's much less sophisticated than that. I just want to put some aside."

"But, why?" asked Elena, lovely in her curiosity, amber eyes wide.

"Well, you know," Giselle confided with mock seriousness. "I am getting older." They both laughed. That was, after all, one of their favorite subjects of conversation. Giselle combing the memories of her mother for menopausal signs to which dates could be assigned: hot flashes, mustaches, higher dry-cleaning bills; Elena enumerating the latest in anti-aging agents: collagen, meditation, vitamin E. "What if . . . just what if Mr. Right comes along, and he wants to have kids, and I can't."

"Oh, don't tell me Mr. Right has finally come along?"

"No, not yet. But he could. And I could be close to the end of my egg-dropping days, and then where would I be?"

"Well, I see your point," said Elena. "Good idea, this egg harvesting. But you know what? I'm hungry. Let's order a Cambodian hot pot, and you can describe the process. Is this something we can talk about while we're eating?"

Giselle didn't know why not. But she also had no idea of what egg harvesting involved. "I can't say," she confessed. "I have to find out more about it."

For the next couple of days, Giselle thought of nothing but eggs. She'd always been fond of them. As a child she'd once stolen a robin's speckled blue egg, a fact that she never recalled without a faint twinge of guilt, although it had bestowed upon her a certain limited popularity among the rest of the members of Mrs. MacFarland's second-grade class at Edinburgh Primary School. Then there was the enormous ostrich egg that had so impressed the girls at Star of the Sea in Athens. Giselle's father had brought it back to her from New Zealand. And of course there were the new baby red eggs that were served at a girl-friend's wedding in Hong Kong. Oh, she'd been carried away by them. They were vinegar-soaked and deep, pinkish red, a symbol of fertility and good luck.

But Giselle's favorite egg memory, one that she cherished more than any other, was of a certain jar of pickled eggs that she'd bought at the Indiana State Fair. The eggs were the work of one Geraldine Feiffer, an ample Indiana housewife with four straw-berry-blonde kids—they were helping her out at the booth. Geraldine had raised the hens that laid the eggs that she used to show off her pickling recipe, and golly, those eggs were good.

This, with a few key omissions, is Geraldine's recipe:

Pickled Eggs

- *Use one dozen eggs.*
- *Place the eggs in a heavy saucepan, cover with water and boil.*
- *Remove eggs, peel them, place in a pickling jar, and add vinegar bath to cover plus one-to-two inches.*
- *Let stand at least one week, opening the jar every day to let the fumes escape.*

Linda Watanabe McFerrin

Vinegar bath:
- *Pour ½ cup vinegar and ¼ cup of water into a saucepan along with one small dried pepper, one clove of garlic, four peppercorns, two whole cloves, and a one-inch piece of ginger root.*
- *Bring to a boil, reduce heat, and simmer five minutes.*
- *Let cool to room temperature before pouring over eggs.*

Giselle never looked at eggs or pickling in quite the same way after she ate Geraldine's. She ate them whole from the jar, with a spoon, on the way out to California. She could even remember where she ate each one of them. She ate one in St. Louis at the county park, studying the Jefferson Barracks diorama. She ate another in Springfield at the Oak Ridge Cemetery. Then she had one as a picnic supper in Tulsa, sitting on the grass right under Oral Roberts's big bronze hands, and another at a truck stop in Amarillo. She ate a pickled egg in Albuquerque and one at Bluewater Lake near the Continental Divide. She ate eggs through the desert all the way to L.A., consuming the very last of her supply on Melrose Avenue in the parking lot outside Fred Segal. Pop. She was ready to try on new clothes.

There were twelve eggs in the jar, a whole dozen, and Giselle's trip from Indiana to L.A. took three days. She ate four eggs a day and not very much else. And she didn't have to stop at a service station restroom once the entire time on the road even though she also drank lots of coffee. Thanks to those eggs, she was tight as a Tupperware bowl. One would think that after three days of pickled eggs, Giselle would never want another, and that was pretty much true, but her fondness for the eggs went way beyond taste. That trip ushered in the best time in her life. Pickled eggs meant a new future. They meant hope.

So with pickled eggs, pink and all-American, on her mind, Giselle logged onto the Net to find out more about what she could do to preserve some of her own. With a click of the streamlined, putty-gray mouse she disappeared into the rabbit hole, into the Black Hole of Calcutta, into the World Wide Web. She keyed in "egg harvesting." This gave her a page full of options that included maternity cults, references to egg symbolism, and selected postings on brine shrimp. For the next hour or so she wandered around in the Wiccan world, learned about brine shrimp and shrimp egg shells, and studied the symbolism on Ukrainian eggs. Waves meant wealth; spirals, the mystery of life and death; meanders stood for harmony, motion, infinity. The pages were red and black and full of dark imagery. She backed out and keyed in "ovum."

"Ovum" gave her life, ovum implantation, and theoretical perambulations about DNA. Ovum implantation led to pregnancy and childbirth, embryology, and sexually-transmitted diseases. Embryology took her to William Harvey, Kaspar Friedrich Wolff, Karl Ernst von Baer, and Theodor Schwann. She wandered through door after door, the mouse leading her further and further afield. She keyed in "artificial insemination" and

Linda Watanabe McFerrin

entered the realm of stud boars and gilts, of swine genetics, of Black Angus and Beefmaster cattle. "Artificial insemination" also led to infertility and the admonitions of Simone de Beauvoir against frivolous childbearing. "Egg donors" led her to online surrogates, notes on testing egg quality, and in vitro fertilization. She read the syrupy confessions and celebrations of women who, for a small sum, had donated their eggs or their bodies. They were all so pleased with what they had done. Bloated with too much information, Giselle clicked onward, finding fertility centers with pink and blue websites featuring photos of well-fertilized families.

Somewhere in the midst of low sperm counts and high levels of follicle stimulator hormones, she came across "assisted reproductive procedure," but the acronyms kept tripping her up. ART involved IVF, GIFT, ZIFT, FET, ICSI, and recommendations from the AMSR. Untangling one strand of information after another she discovered that Assisted Reproductive Therapy involved In Vitro Fertilization, Gamete Intra-Fallopian Transfer, Zygote Intra-Fallopian Transfer, and so on. Harvesting eggs meant stimulating the body to produce a clutch instead of the usual one and then plucking them from the ovaries, ideally for immediate use. In Giselle's case, and in the case of anyone saving up for a rainy day, the next step wasn't fertilization, but cryopreservation. The eggs were frozen and stored. Giselle imagined little white refrigerators filled with itsy-bitsy, test-tube-sized cartons of minuscule eggs, but reality was slightly more clinical. Deep-frozen eggs, sperm, and embryos, she learned, were kept not in kitchens but in banks.

By the time she got to cryopreservation, Giselle had developed a headache. There was something mildly disturbing about banks full of fast-frozen pieces of human procreation waiting around for withdrawal. Then there were the storage fees; even an ovum has to pay rent. And disposal instructions. What do you do with the stuff no one wants? Giselle put one hand on her stomach and took down the phone number and address of the closest fertility clinic. Perhaps a real visit would make the whole process seem a bit more humane. She would ask Elena to join her.

Pacific Coast Laboratories and Fertility Centers was headquartered in a quiet Santa Monica suburb. A long, flat cakebox of a building, it had palm trees and a pebbled walkway in front that reminded Giselle of the Flintstones. Inside it was white with a terra-cotta-colored linoleum floor that made the white corridors and waiting rooms look wider still.

"This place is exceedingly strange," Elena remarked, tossing her mane of honey-blonde hair with a snort that was vaguely equestrian. She was wearing black capri pants, a short faux-leopard jacket, and harlequin sunglasses so that no one would recognize her. Of course, this turned heads and set people to wondering who she actually was. Giselle's tall, thin frame was suited in red. Red that contrasted sharply with the fair hue of her skin and the corn-colored blonde hair cut to fan out at the side of her face, just under her chin. High-heeled black shoes and an enormous

Linda Watanabe McFerrin

black bag completed an ensemble that made her look, in the context of that albumin-colored clinic, as exotic as a Tutsi princess.

Elena was right. It was an odd place. There were four or five other couples filling out forms and waiting in the wide reception area, all looking uncomfortable and colorlessly lumpy as they leaned into one another and squirmed on their beige vinyl seats.

"Here we are amidst the infertile," whispered Elena dramatically as they took their chairs in the waiting room along with the others, Giselle with a tablet of forms to fill out. Elena's amber eyes flitted inquisitively from one person to the next. "It simply boggles the mind," she observed.

Two by two, like applicants for a spot on the ark, the clingy couples around them were called to shuffle off into offices and consultations.

"I'll bet they're thinking we're gay," guessed Elena, winking at a pasty fellow and his extra-wide wife who'd risen to the nurse's latest summons.

"Very likely," Giselle replied absently. She'd just finished filling out the forms. "Partner's Information," they'd prompted. She'd written "TBD" on every line.

"Do you think they'll hold being single against me?"

"I don't see why they would," Elena responded thoughtfully. "Every case is different, you know."

Giselle liked how that sounded. Elena never had doubts. She took the world at face value. She expected it to make sense. That was why Giselle had asked her best friend to accompany her.

Minutes ticked tediously by.

"Ms. McFee," the reception room nurse finally announced.

To the highly colorized speculation of everyone else present, the extravagant pair jumped up and followed her out of the room.

Dr. Spitch registered a small tremor of shock—around 2.0 on his personal Richter Scale—when the two women entered his office. Perhaps it was pleasure or maybe relief at the prospect of a break in another monotonous mauve and blue day. He adjusted his glasses and straightened his tie.

"So, tell me how we can help you, Ms. McFee," he inquired, a little too eagerly Giselle thought, once she and Elena had folded themselves into the prickly, low-slung chairs.

Giselle rambled on about menopause and her mother and Mr. Right for a while. "I'm single, but hopeful," she concluded. "Not your usual client, I suspect."

"Well, every case is different," the doctor assured putting on his most worldly-wise voice.

Elena's golden irises shot out beams. "That's just what I said," she enthused, her sienna-red mouth wide and smiling.

"Really?" The doctor's head snapped toward her, Giselle forgotten, the feline Elena filling his mind. He turned almost painfully back to Giselle. "I'm certain Mr. Right will come along for you," he consoled with an eye toward Elena. "As far as the procedure goes: we begin with a pelvic exam, then a series of Lupron injections. I have here a booklet that explains it all in detail. You should study it closely, and if you feel you want to

Linda Watanabe McFerrin

move forward, schedule an appointment, and we'll begin."

"That's it?" asked Giselle.

"Yes. Quite." Dr. Spitch closed the interview with a warm smile meant to include them both.

"No psychological tests?"

"Well, no. Not in your case. There are no surrogates involved. Your decision involves no one else."

"No one else," Giselle repeated sorrowfully.

"No one else at this time!" Dr. Spitch chirped back.

"At this time," stressed Elena, patting the top of her friend's red-fingernailed hand.

In a move of great gallantry, Dr. Spitch stood when Giselle and Elena got up to leave, realizing too late his error, looking up at the tall women, the inadequacy of his genetics all too clearly exposed.

"Good day," he said stiffly, extending his hand.

Giselle shook it with her pale one.

"Bye, Doc." Elena smiled down at him.

"Oh my God, that doctor was smarmy," Giselle shuddered as they slid back into her car. "Imagine the pelvic exam."

"Not the physician for you, I suspect," laughed Elena as Giselle swung the Saab gracefully out of its parking space. "A bit too eager, I think."

"Eager for you, maybe. That man was auditioning for a part in your life."

"Not in my life," mumbled Elena, her voice barely audible under the purr of the vehicle's air-conditioning. "Speaking of life, can we please shelve this part of your project for a bit? Let's take on a much more satisfying piece of the equation. Herbert Octel is giving a party. Why don't we go there and schmooze, Giselle? You haven't been to a party in ages."

"I'll think about it," Giselle promised, dropping back into her thoughts. The car sped along, hugging the Santa Monica Freeway.

Although not a physician, Elena was right. The best possible prescription for Giselle's dilemma was a good party. Giselle hadn't been to a party in a very long time, and that probably had something to do with moping. Moping was the attire that Giselle's worries favored. She moped as easily as some women put on a little black dress. Lately she'd been moping over "there is no Mr. Right," and every Mr. Wrong she met became one more crack in the fairy tale. She'd decided that one way to cut down on encounters with Mr. Wrong was to not go out. So Giselle had recently taken to keeping herself to herself in the hope that fewer wrongs would eventually yield a right. But with that social strategy, the only men she encountered were waiters and pizza-delivery boys who unfairly seemed to further swell the Mr. Wrong ranks. Scrapping her obviously misguided plans, she made up her mind that Herbert's party would be just the thing, and replacing her mopey garb with a Chinese dress of celery-green silk, she showed up on the wide, white verandah of Herbert's Beverly Hills estate.

For Giselle, the party was like a debut. She'd been out of circulation so long that there was a nearly audible gasp from the room full of friends and acquaintances when she walked in the door.

Linda Watanabe McFerrin

"Giselle, I'd heard you were ill," Herbert crooned in greeting as he sandwiched one of her hands between his velvety pair.

"No, Herbert. I'm fine," Giselle said, looking waifish, the celery color of her dress very vegetal and shy against the grandeur and stark contrasts of Herbert's home.

The dining room was raised, the living room sunken, and out beyond the window-framed front deck, the night sky gleamed like a pitch-colored ocean fretted with herring-bright stars. Candles flickered everywhere, lighting up Herbert's collection of silver milagros, and licking at the large pieces of ocean salvage situated around the rooms. The house was carpeted in white, curtained in sepia. Large poufs in black and sepia striping added a fanciful, candy-like touch.

Circulating like busy black wasps were the waiters, their silver trays loaded with exotic canapés, martinis, and tall flutes of champagne.

"Well, I'm so glad you've come," Herbert said kindly. "Everyone else will be, too," he added, indicating the rest of the room.

Giselle nodded, scanning the familiar faces. Elena gave a queenly wave from her post near the fireplace, delight flashing across her features. She was wearing a short dress of gold lace and stiletto heels that made her taller than almost all of the men. Patrick, Aaron, Drew—Giselle counted lots of pals and old loves. There were so many—Mr. Wrong, Mr. Wrong—the pageant of her past blowing kisses across the room.

Eyes moving from one memory to another she ran into an

unfamiliar visage, an intelligence that assessed her just as she was sizing up everyone else. Standing empty-handed and, by this time, alone, Giselle felt naked. The gang of worries stopped what they were doing as though caught in the act and took note.

She couldn't help staring at the man as he stared at her. Eyes fixed on her target, she took inventory. He was six-foot-four-inches, she guessed, which meant he was taller than she. Big brown eyes. Dark brows. A square jaw. Wide shoulders. He looked conservative in a dark coat and slacks, but he wore a colorful tie and a marvelous pair of loafers that looked more like slippers than shoes. But the best part, the very best part, the part that made the fine gold filaments that dusted certain parts of her body stand on end, was that he was as bald as an egg.

"Daddy Warbucks," she breathed in her fantasy world. In her dream, he smiled at her and beckoned.

"So what do you think?" he asked Giselle when she walked up to him.

"About . . . ?"

"About me," he laughed. "I felt like a vase at an auction."

"Oh, I think you're splendid," Giselle replied. *Splendid?* Why did she have to say *splendid?*

"Splendid," he repeated, sending the word up over the room like a kite. "Ah, splendid. Well, there's more. Shall we talk?"

It sounded so much like "shall we dance" that Giselle nodded and held out her hand, which he took, guiding her gently into a wonderful waltz of words; a whirl with a dervish; a pas de

Linda Watanabe McFerrin

deux with a lovely, bald prince; a swirling carousel, feet-off-the-ground twirl with the Daddy Warbucks of suitors, the Siamese king, the magical, fairy tale egg man.

"Have you always been bald?" Giselle queried, trying to do it politely. She couldn't resist the question.

"No," he replied somewhat shyly. "I had hair as a boy, of course. But as I got older, it got thinner, so I finally shaved it all off." He ran one large hand over the top of his head. "But I like it."

"So do I," sang Giselle, looking at the gleaming dome under his hand. "Your head is really quite . . . splendid."

By this point, Giselle's worries had all donned tutus and sequins. They were romping around like sugarplum fairies full of cheer and great expectations. She sailed with the egg prince up over the crowd and away—back past her mother's illness and adult disappointments; back past school, childhood traumas and fears; back to the time when she was no more than a happy and hopeful ovum.

"Giselle," asked the egg prince, "what are you thinking?" He was watching an impish, almost naughty smile dance over her face.

"I was thinking about how I used to worry about things," said Giselle, one hand like a flower on his dark lapel. "I don't have to, do I?"

"Of course not," he laughed. "Let's say all of your problems are solved." His dark eyes seemed to twinkle like the starlit night.

"Can we go for a ride?" she asked suddenly.

"Certainly," answered the prince of eggs.

"And what kind of car do you happen to have?"

"A Mercedes convertible. I hope it will do. And you? What kind of car do you drive?"

"I have a little white Saab," Giselle answered primly. "Let's take your car."

They drove with the top down and the stars at their crowns. Giselle could not feel the road beneath them. They climbed into the hills, the egg prince parked the car, and they sat gazing over a city spread like emeralds, rubies, and diamonds all the way to the sea—bright as a Mexican print on black velvet.

"It's amazing," she whispered.

"Yes, it is," said the prince, one arm draped over her shoulders.

"I think you are beautiful," Giselle confessed, suddenly grave. She laid one hand gently on the top of his head. "The most beautiful man in the world."

"Thank you," said the egg man, once again seeming shy.

"And I'll bet you like children, too," she said slyly.

"Yes, I do," he replied.

"Are you going to have kids one day?" *Mr. Right,* she wanted to say.

"Not anymore," said the prince of eggs, the lord of dervishes, the king of Siam. "I have three little girls from a previous marriage—Corin, Celia, and Colette. That's enough for me. I have plenty."

Giselle found herself in the mirror of his eyes. "Oh," she heard herself saying simply.

The egg prince felt the change in the wind. "It's time to get

Linda Watanabe McFerrin

you home," he murmured.

By the time he took Giselle back to her car, the night had nearly disappeared, pearly dawn nudging up underneath it.

"You know," he said to Giselle as he helped her out of his automobile, "I would call you, but I think I should leave that decision up to you."

Giselle nodded and took his hand in hers. "Thank you so much," she said as the worries shook their mournful heads and sat back on their haunches. "I really had a wonderful time."

"Splendid?" he asked.

"Yes. Splendid."

Giselle's hand hovered over the gray oval of the mouse.

For the past few days she'd been moping. That morning, in the kitchen, just happening to glance at the chicken-wire basket full of eggs that sat on the counter, she broke down into tears. In her mind, one worry limped around and around in a circle.

She'd met Mr. Right, and he didn't want children. But she wasn't sure she didn't. And what if she did? Then he'd be one more Mr. Wrong. But maybe that wasn't the issue. Maybe the issue was relationships. That sent her mind into a tailspin. *What did she want?*

She sat back in her chair, finger gently tapping the mouse.

"Sperm donors," she thought, mentally launching the search.

Or should she simply call up the egg man?

Childproofing

The house was huge. Inside, white like a conch, like bone. Outside, the color of sand. Claire felt like a whelk within it, invisible to the casual eye, thinly veiled by the powder of rock, ground glass-fine. It was what they had worked for—this ostentatious hiding place on a hill at the end of a cul-de-sac in one of the most expensive counties in the most expensive state in the most expensive country in the world.

This was not the house Claire had grown up in. Not even close. The house that had cradled and cuddled Claire through her childhood was the yellow of egg yolk fading to cream. She was no longer certain of the color of the walls inside. They were, in her memory, rosebud with dawn, corn and cornflower through the long, hot Nebraska summers, pumpkin for ever-so-long in the evening when the days began to shorten, moonlit blue and well-black through the star-bright nights. And sometimes when powerhouse storms pushed in over the countryside, the walls turned the color of the wind and rain—gray and silver, charcoal and lead.

Claire's old house was old indeed. It had been built by a great-great-grandfather to sustain a family out on the plains—

a family that was its own community. He had given the house a wraparound porch with doors on three sides that swung open and shut all day as parents and children and dogs and cats and flies and mosquitoes danced out and in, out and in. Beneath it he had excavated a cellar, the strongbox for all that he cherished, with more doors out and in. Four hundred yards from the side-door entrance, he had built a barn which he filled with animals. And he dug a well and made a pond where children and pets and insects and frogs would gather in a boisterous tangle through the decades ahead.

The house was, in many ways, the most important part of Claire's family. It was as if it were the oldest living and most venerable member of their clan. It had held them safe through disasters, both natural and man-made. It had witnessed tantrums and traumas and incredible reconciliations. There was always an armchair close at hand to collapse into or a big table around which the family could gather three times a day and then some. It was full of memories and furniture and people. Not like Claire's sand-colored house at the end of the cul-de-sac, which was new, sparsely furnished, and held only two.

When she was very young Claire had thought of that old, yellow house as a castle. Later, after college took her away for a while and relatives urged her to "come back," she saw it as a prison. Recently, it had taken on a new character in her mind. It was a sanctuary, an asylum of peace floating in a moat of farmland somewhere in the middle kingdom of her mind.

Linda Watanabe McFerrin

It was the weight of the dolphins that brought Claire back to that Friday night in her living room. She stood in her socks in the center of the dark hardwood floor that gleamed like a pool of molasses oozing out for twenty feet in every direction. In her arms she held a trinity of bronze dolphins, released just moments before from their newspaper wrappings. The large piece was a housewarming present from Doug's parents, who lived in a home not unlike the one that Claire and their son, Douglas Allen, had finally settled into. For twelve years Douglas and Claire had lived in apartments, and Doug's parents had worried that their only son and his wife would never take life seriously. The style and dimensions of the couple's new home were a sign of just how seriously they did take it. Doug's parents breathed a joint sigh of relief. The dolphins were purchased in celebration of their good fortune—theirs, not Douglas and Claire's.

Claire realized as she stood bowed slightly backward, the red-brown dolphins balancing on arms against her chest, that she had been lost in thought, wool-gathering as her mother would have called it. She had heard the splash as children and pets leapt into the pond. She could almost feel the water slurping up to her face. And what was that funny thump, thump? Carefully sliding along the polished floor in her cotton socks, trying hard not to let her legs slip out from under the weight of the sculpture, Claire made her way to the white Berber carpet that blanketed the hall, and then, on steadier ground, positioned herself in front of the console table in the entry vestibule. She was just getting ready to ease the dolphins up onto the rich veneer of its surface when she heard it again. The odd thump, thump.

The sound, which she was suddenly certain was not in her mind, seemed to be coming from beyond the French doors that led to the back stone terrace. The noise was small, unidentifiable, and quite out of context, and so it sickened and frightened her. She considered the possibilities. Children climbing the fence with mischief in mind. A tree limb snapped and drumming against something—what? A person back there, maybe snooping, maybe planning to break in. Something that had come from the forest.

The back of the house had a fence, a high one on two sides, with nothing between the edge of the property and the forested hillside. Beyond those French doors was the stone terrace, the pool, the wide sweep of lawn, flower beds, an herb garden, and the hillside: spindly chaparral, manzanita, bay laurel, eucalyptus, and oak. The pool was new. Doug had it built right after they bought the house and before they moved in. Olympic-sized, just like the one at his parents' home.

Claire, still embracing the heavy gift, had been holding her breath. Exhaling slowly, she pushed the dolphin sculpture up onto the top of the console table and shoved it wallward. Two fine scratches appeared on the wood, running parallel like ski tracks right up to where three bronze dolphins leapt from the sea. Turning toward the French doors, she felt her stomach turn over and rise up through her chest until she could feel it crowding her lungs, fighting its way to the base of her throat. She crept

Linda Watanabe McFerrin

through the house in her stocking feet, and then, although she suspected that it was probably the wrong thing to do, she threw on the back light and flooded the terrace in the synthetic brilliance of three two-hundred-watt halogen bulbs. Then, knowing that this, undoubtedly, was also a terribly wrong move, she unlocked the door and stepped out onto the terrace.

Eight o'clock on an August night, the warmth that met her as she stepped into it was something of a surprise. Doug was working late at the office or the lab or wherever he had decided to spend his long day. The artificial light sluiced down toward the stone terrace and poolward, joining the lights there to ignite the rectangle of water into a gemstone, a brilliant aquamarine. Aquamarine with a mote, however, a dark blot floating, floating, twitching a little, floating, floating, drifting toward the shallower terrace side. Claire, without thinking, ran down the terrace steps, over the round stones in her socks, not feeling the rocks or anything, knowing what it was lying on the pool's surface, knowing the shape of it as surely as she knew her childhood, the feeling of her arms around a creature new or old, small or large, its breath soft and steamy and secret in her hair.

The deer was not dead yet. That was impossible. Claire knew this as she knelt at the side of the pool, reached out, tried to pull it toward her, touched its warm flank, felt the velvet nap of fur, smelled the fuzzy, earthy, mushroomy, animal smell, as the water, insisting, took it further away from her. She jumped in after it, standing in the shallow end, tugging it toward her, trying to keep the head aloft, the black eye bright in the halogen light, reflecting life, she thought. It shivered, came alive in her arms, and she towed it to the side and tried to lift it—oh, it was so heavy, so much heavier than the dolphins—and she put her back into it or tried to, but she couldn't, couldn't lift it up to the edge. And she understood that she wouldn't be able to get it up and out, tears pouring into the pool as she slipped, and its head broke the surface, going under again, and its eyes were dark now, and its weight heavier still, heavy and stiff, so that she knew she was pushing around a dead thing. But she couldn't give up so she pushed and cried and pushed and cried, putting her face up onto its face, cheek to cheek, dog-paddling and weeping next to the dark, floating form.

The deer still lay, dead, on its chlorinated bed as Claire ran the peach towel over her hair and body. She put on dry clothes and, barefoot, padded over to the phone to call Douglas. She tried his office first. Then she tried the lab, listening to the telephone beg into the silence. So easy to ignore, that sound. Doug would not answer the call if he were involved in a project. He'd let it ring and ring.

Claire remembered how a different phone had bleated into the void on that afternoon a year and a half ago when she had called her mother. The house in Nebraska was empty, the family gathered around a woman in a hospital bed who had become as transparent as the tubes leading into her violet veins, whose three sons would become pallbearers escorting her to the rectangle of ground that was her bequest. Doug had accompanied Claire to

Linda Watanabe McFerrin

the funeral. He wore black slacks and a black collared sweater. No tie. He grew impatient with the towheaded nieces and nephews banging in and out of the screen doors, bumping into the adults who swarmed like tired flies in the pale, yellow house. He read on the plane on the way out, then again on the way back.

Claire dropped the receiver into its cradle. She went to her workroom and took a seat at her drafting table. The lamp dropped a full moon of light onto the pearl-white paper. Claire scratched a crosshatch of hair-fine black lines into the back of a ruddy duck, destined to adorn household linens or ties, that bobbed on the right-hand side of the page. Headlights. A car pulling into the drive. The front door opening.

"Claire? I thought I'd find you in here. You know, you're going to go blind in this light."

Claire squinted up at her husband. "I tried to call you at the lab," she said, surprised at how indifferent she could make her voice sound. "You must have been on your way home. There's a dead deer in the pool in the back."

"Jane Doe or John Doe?" he quipped with a grin, not understanding, not sensing the gravity of her remark. He noted, too late, the thin line of her lips, an expression that could be construed as cruel.

"I don't know. Why don't you find out for yourself."

Claire's gaze was stony. He could tell she was angry. That was all right. He could deal with anger and indifference. They were sentiments he could contend with.

There was, indeed, a dead deer in the pool. Coastal blacktail, a doe, and from the look of her around 120 pounds. Doug considered fishing her out, then thought better of it. The doe might be diseased. He called the police who called Animal Control. They shared his concern. Late as it was, they'd send somebody out. Doug hung up the phone, poured two glasses of wine, and took them back to Claire's workroom.

"Was it dead when you found it?"

"Yes," Claire lied.

"I called Animal Control. They're sending somebody out. I'm going to put up another fence," he added, handing a glass of wine to Claire.

Claire took the wine. "Fine," she said. She didn't want to discuss the deer. The deer was connected to a sunken line of invisible woes. She didn't want to raise them. The brittle resentment into which she retreated lent a dark little comfort. Doug would handle the dead deer with fences and Animal Control. He'd push happily back at anger and resistance. If she mentioned the loss and longing that had wrapped itself around her heart, he would buckle. And then he would distance himself, run as far and fast as he could. That's what he'd done in all of his other relationships. Claire didn't want to be one more failure in an ongoing series. She kept her dreams to herself. She adapted. That's how their marriage survived.

"I'm going to bed," she said carelessly. "It's too late for dinner. I'll let you deal with Animal Control."

Linda Watanabe McFerrin

The men who came to pick up the doe arrived after midnight. There were six of them wearing blue twill coveralls. They clattered around at the front door and dragged their equipment through the house over the white Berber carpets and hardwood floors instead of using the outdoor easement. They set up a winch to hoist out the deer, but they still couldn't get the animal up and over the side of the pool. The legs of the deer were entangled in some kind of debris. There were tree root tentacles wrapped around her legs. Perhaps that was why she had fallen into the water and drowned. The men increased the winch tension, the deer's hip pulled from its socket, and all of the animal except the one leg rose from the water to hang suspended a few feet above it for a moment or two. Then they yanked her up higher, that last leg emerging, trailing roots and paper and three or four towheaded children. Doug put his hands over his face and backed onto the terrace where his parents waited with two glasses of wine to comfort him. They shook their heads sadly while the men cut the deer down and loaded her into a sling. Then the workmen dragged the doe to the front of the house, this time using the easement, packed everything into their van, and sped off into the night. Doug and his parents must have left, too, because Claire was completely alone. She ran through the rooms hunting for Doug and crying while the telephone wailed like a lonely old woman into her empty home.

It was the alarm clock, not the phone, that awakened her. Claire lifted her head from the pillow and turned. Doug was

Childproofing   175 sleeping peacefully beside her, sunlight streaming in through the window, dappling his face in small lemon coins. Claire went to the window. The clear and unblemished face of the swimming pool twinkled up at her. Abashed by her dream, she regarded her face in the dressing room mirror. A pair of troubled green eyes, cupped in puffy half-moons of gray shadow, gazed back at her. Reproachfully, she dressed and headed down to the kitchen to scramble eggs and make amends.

Doug built the fence as he'd promised. What was one more wall? Pleased that he'd so efficiently handled the problem, he swam in the pool, ate meals at the table on the terrace beside it, and forgot about the deer and the drowning. He assumed Claire had, too. But she hadn't.

Claire just didn't trust the fence. She was the pool security system, keeping watch over the tricky rectangle, making sure roots, ropes, hoses, anything that a creature could trip on, were neatly stowed away. Every day she scanned the hillside for deer, her eyes roaming the slow climb of brush for the dapple-gray forms. She'd see them standing, stock still and almost invisible in chaparral, gazing intently back at her. Sometimes she'd stand at the bedroom window for hours, watching the deer graze the brakes.

It would be hard to say what made the gap in the fence. Maybe the deer or some other animal worried a weak spot where the boards were loose and too distantly spaced until it finally gave way. It wasn't a large hole, but it was big enough. Big enough for a fawn to slip easily through. Big enough for a

Linda Watanabe McFerrin

doe, though she might push till her flanks were bloodstained and raw, to be trapped in.

This time Claire, working in her office midday, ears tuned to the pool, heard the splash and knew what it was. She ran, sprinting down stairs, over carpet, hardwood, and stone toward the sound. The size of the creature thrashing at the deep end of the pool reassured her. She could do this. Catapulting into the water feet first, legs like scissors, arms sweeping down through blue resistance, she made the deep end in almost a moment, then dove, looking up through the drift of aquamarine to the shadowy struggle above her. In slow motion she regarded the four legs kicking helplessly under the fawn's tiny body—fast, hard, hard, fast—fiercely trying to walk on water. She swam up and around to approach at its flank and avoid the smack of its hooves. Quickly, so quickly it could not wriggle free, she entwined it, immobilizing one leg as she rolled it toward her, her face in its neck, mouth next to the delicate spade of its ear, so close she could fill it with secrets. Its hind legs rebelled, whipping violently backward. Claire felt a sudden flash of pain in her shin as she tightened her grip, the tired fawn going slack as she swam it to the shallower side.

Stroking to where she could stand in the pool and use the steps to support the fawn's legs, Claire maneuvered the animal's body carefully into position and tried to heave the forty-pound burden up and out of the water. The fawn, sensing safety, came savagely to life, twisting in Claire's arms, swinging back its head and hitting her in the jaw. Claire felt the hammer of a hoof on her shoulder as the animal scrambled onto dry land. The fawn fell to its knees, where it stayed for a moment, as though praying, before fighting its way to its feet. It stood shakily, dripping wet and in shock, its four legs trembling as if it wanted to strike out at once in all four different directions. Then, from beyond the back fence, came an odd ululation, and the fawn turned its head and trotted wearily toward it.

The doe had somehow managed to wrestle free from the gap in the fence and now only her muzzle protruded as she called to her young one from the opposite side. Small bits of blood and fur were stuck to the wood where her body had been wedged. The fawn hurried toward the soft gun of warmth that reached through the fence toward it. Dark noses met. The mother started licking and licking, and the fawn, bowing head and neck to the pink washcloth of tongue, squirmed back through the gap to its mother.

Exhausted, Claire climbed from the pool. Her shoulder complained in a wave of pain as she grabbed the sides of the ladder. She could suddenly feel the dull throb of her jaw. It hurt when she opened her mouth. One water-soaked pant leg was stuck to her shin. Nausea washed over her as she pulled it up over her knee. There was a deep cut in her leg where the deer had kicked her. She didn't want to look closely, but she thought she discerned the white flash of bone. After limping back to the house, Claire tried to call Doug. No answer. No answer. She dialed up a neighbor, then peeled off her clothes, put on dry ones, and waited for someone to come and take her to the emergency room.

Linda Watanabe McFerrin

Somewhere along the line, Claire passed out. She remembered sitting on a gurney and chatting with the emergency room nurse, who was pleasant and gave her a couple of shots. The next thing she knew she was lying down on the gurney. Then a doctor came into the room. The doctor smiled down at her and began poking at her shin. He asked Claire what had happened. Claire started to tell him. She felt sleepy and relaxed and pleasantly numb. She told him about the deer, first the one that had drowned, then the one that had kicked her.

"Little deer like a baby," she mumbled drowsily through the fog that was settling deliciously over her.

"A deer, eh?" the doctor grinned back. "Well, sometimes these creatures carry diseases, so I'm going to give you a couple of shots. Just a precaution. Then we'll stitch you right up."

"Mmmm, precaution," Claire repeated as her mind started sewing up the wound in her leg, started mending a fence, tried to remember to do one more thing. One more thing. What was it? What was it?

The doctor turned to the nurse. "Has her husband been called?"

The nurse nodded a definitive "yes."

"Claire, what have you done to yourself?" Doug exclaimed when he arrived at the emergency room. The lower right side of Claire's face was swollen and bruised. Her shoulder was wrapped. The front of her shin was taped up with surgical gauze.

"Baby deer," she muttered through a Vicoden haze. Her jaw did not want to open. Doug stiffened and took a step back, pulled away. That is what Claire saw. In spite of the Vicoden, she felt a poker of anger push up from her gut.

"Yes, I know about that, the doctor explained it." His question had been merely rhetorical. "I guess it got through the fence."

"I don't want that pool there," Claire hissed through her bruises. She wanted to reach out and slap him.

"Look, Claire, let me get you home," said Douglas, commandeering a wheelchair and helping her to the car with surprising tenderness.

The ride home was silent. Claire fell asleep. Doug drove, eyes on the road, mind on the woman curled up next to him.

Claire took drugs and sulked through the next couple of days, working very little. Her right arm ached, slowing her output. The soreness in her jaw, her shoulder, and her shin got worse, then subsided, but the poker of anger that had stirred in her gut grew more violent. She would stand, teeth clenched, at the bedroom window, looking down on the pool and the fence that Douglas had patched.

The pool was a blue coffin waiting to be filled. She could measure her loss in it. And the fence? Ignorance. Just one more attempt to try to shut out the truth. She was an imposter hiding in an alien shell. Doug's shell and his parents'. What had happened to her life, her home? Where, for that matter, was Claire? From the brush-covered hillside, the deer looked critically back at her.

Doug came home later and later from work. It happened that Claire's "accident,"—that's what he called it in spite of the fact that the events that led to her injuries could not have been more deliberate—coincided with the looming deadline for a very large project. The project was running behind schedule. Nothing he was doing at the lab was yielding the proper results, procedures that had worked so well in the past weren't getting him anywhere. At night, even at home, he found himself absently running over assumptions. Then there was Claire. She was different. It was as though she'd packed some invisible bags and set them by the door. She had her coat on and one eye on the pool. Anger he could contend with, but between them, her rage was a wide flume of sorrow. He could feel himself shrinking away from it.

Claire couldn't stop thinking about the pool. And the deer. And Doug. And her marriage. "Look," she said to Doug on the night before the stitches came out of her shin, "I don't want that pool back there anymore. Too many deer have fallen in."

"Two deer, Claire." Doug stated the obvious.

"Two deer," Claire repeated. "Two deer aren't enough?" She cocked her head strangely. "Very well," she said primly, lips slightly pursed. "I see where you stand on the matter. By the way, Doug," she added tilting up the bruised jaw—Doug saw that the purple had become marbled chartreuse—"have you ever noticed how you seem to make all of the rules. Our marriage is very unbalanced."

"Oh, we have rules?" Doug asked, lifting his brows.

"Yes, we do," affirmed Claire, feeling suddenly foolish, like a woman who was making up lies. "Yes, we certainly do." She could feel the tears starting in the corners of her eyes.

Doug could feel it, too, the rising swell of Claire's sorrow. "Look," he said, "we're both really tired. I'm going to bed now. You come on up when you're ready." He made a hasty escape.

Claire didn't follow, and Doug fell asleep, his breath deep and regular in the darkness. He awoke to scraping and clatter. The backyard was lit up like Christmas. He rushed to the window. In the garish light below he saw Claire, standing next to the pool in a sweatsuit and rainboots. Her hair was tied back as it was when she slept. She had two or three shovels around her. There were six large troughs cut into the lawn and from each of them a dark runway of grassy soil trailed up to and into the water. On the turquoise blue surface the black earth floated like coffee grounds. As he watched, Claire sprang back into action, dragging one of the shovels back toward her divots, widening them further and yelling.

"I am sick of this pool," she shouted into the night. "And I care about deer and people."

"That's it," muttered Doug, and he marched down the stairs. "Claire," he hissed from the terrace, "come inside."

"Why?" Claire asked, eyes full of tears, swinging the shovel over her shoulder. It still ached where the deer's hoof had caught her. "So that I can pretend nothing's wrong? There's no one home at our house, Doug. Nobody home at all. What we have is this puddle of selfishness and a bunch of dead deer." She tore

Linda Watanabe McFerrin

her eyes from her husband's face and tried to address the furrow at her feet, but the strength had gone out of her. She felt helpless and spent. She was weeping.

This time Doug knew better than to remind his wife of the actual number of deer. "I'm so sorry, Claire," he said regarding the disheveled woman who was crying over her shovel. His eyes wandered over the potholed lawn, past the flower beds, over the fence, and up the hillside to where trees hummed and shushed in the breeze-laden night. Everything in the back was in wild disarray. Mounds of earth and grass pimpled the lawn. Gashes ran deep and wide over its contours. He had no idea what to do for Claire. An infuriating feeling of powerlessness was bullying its way through his body. He recoiled from it, but it persisted. Running his hands through his hair and shaking his head, Doug stalked back into the house.

They didn't talk after that. Doug left the house early. Claire knew she'd upset him. She drew back the curtain and looked down on the yard. What a mess. It looked like demented gophers had attacked it. Like a very bad joke, one she couldn't take back, it laughed up at her. There were no deer on the hillside. Claire thought that perhaps they'd deserted her, too. Face burning with regret, she checked the time and got dressed. She had one business meeting, then she'd go to the hospital, where the doctor would remove her stitches.

Coming home from the hospital, Claire knew that something was wrong the moment she pulled onto her street. Up ahead, corralled in the cul-de-sac in front of her home, was a welter of yellow equipment. Two men in blue jeans were barking instructions. Four more swarmed the trucks, and tractors blocked the drive and front walkways.

"What is this?" asked Claire as she pulled up and got out of her car.

"Excuse me, ma'am, your car is going to be in the way there," one of the men in blue advised her.

"Look," she snapped back, "this is *my* house. Just what are you men doing here?"

"Oh, Claire, you must be Claire," the man answered, very pleased.

"Hey, guys, she's finally here. This is Claire."

The other men stopped whatever it was they were doing and walked slowly over to Claire. They gathered in almost a circle around her, hands on their hips, smiles on all of their raggedy faces. Six sets of eyes were upon her—pale blue, hazel, brown, brown, blue, pale blue. Claire's hands instinctively tightened. She made two fists full of the fabric of her skirt. "What are you here for?" she heard herself ask.

"We're here for you, Claire," said the man with blue eyes. Claire thought he must be the leader. "You are the reason for this."

"Yeah," said one of the men with brown eyes. "Now that you're here we can start."

The men were all watching her closely, still smiling, still standing, hands on their hips. They moved just a little closer to Claire, eagerly maybe, bringing the circle in a tiny bit tighter.

Linda Watanabe McFerrin

"But I didn't call you," Claire whispered. "And I don't want you here, understand? Would you leave? Just leave. I really want you to go."

"We can't just go, Claire," the man with blue eyes argued.

"Why not?" Claire wailed.

"Because, we have orders," he explained. The others nodded their heads and grinned broadly. "Look," he reasoned, pushing back his cap. Claire suddenly noted they were all wearing caps. "Look, we need to get started, so you're going to have to help us. We have all this equipment." He gestured back toward the front of the house, the driveway, the yard where the big machines hunched like mechanical locusts. "And we cannot do this without you."

"Do what without me?" Claire screamed. "I don't know you, any of you. And you don't know me. I didn't call you. I have no idea why you're here." Claire cast her eyes toward the house, realized she was looking at it through a filmy curtain of tears.

"Ma'am . . . " the man with hazel eyes stepped toward her.

"Get away from me," Claire yelled at him. "Don't touch me. Don't any of you touch me. I don't know why you're here. I'm not the person who called you. Can't you just, please, leave me alone?" she whimpered. She was crying overtly, tears waterfalling over her cheeks.

The men looked troubled, looked back over their shoulders at all the bright yellow equipment.

"Don't you understand?" she implored between sobs. "I am not responsible for your presence. Who are you? Who sent you? Why the hell are you here?"

All six men's raggedy faces looked shocked. The man with blue eyes was frowning.

"I'm sorry, I'm so sorry," he said softly. "I thought you knew we'd be here."

"How, how would I know?" Claire sniveled, wiping her nose on her wrist.

"We were told you'd be really pleased. That you'd be happy to see us." The six men nodded in agreement, their capped heads rising and falling.

"Happy?" Claire squeaked.

"Yeah," said the blue-eyed man with a wide smile. "Doug, Mr. Allen, sent us. We're here to fill in the pool."

Khalida's Dog

I'm not a romantic person. I'm a theoretical mathematician, which means I like numbers, and even though the theoretical part gets a little preposterous at times, I can prove everything I surmise. Still, I'm always intrigued by things I just can't explain. I'm an absolute sucker for magic. Take Circe, for example. Circe was a witch who lived on an island in the Ionian Sea. According to Homer, the ancient Greek poet, Circe would give sailors who were shipwrecked on her island an enchanted brew that turned them into pigs. It almost happened to Odysseus on his way home to Ithaca, but the crafty man got away. His companions didn't. They were turned into swine. Some women have that effect on men. Today, when we call somebody a Circe it means she's a dangerous and irresistibly fascinating woman. Khalida is just such a gal.

On Thursday evenings six of us head independently to Khalida's studio in the Berkeley hills where she teaches her beginning belly dancing class. We're supposed to arrive at around 7:00 P.M. We climb a wide flight of peeling red stairs to a rambling shingle house and stand at the door. On the other side of the door we hear a dog bark. The dog always barks. He barks at each and every one of us before we enter, and he continues to bark a few more times after we come in. He is a big black dog, long-haired, very attractive, and looks to be a combination of a retriever and a setter. Sometimes he is accompanied by another student who has opened the door for us. Sometimes he is accompanied by Khalida. Regardless of who accompanies him, he barks his greeting. Sometimes Khalida says, "Solo, no. Shhhh," and she bends down to him just a bit, letting her soft white breasts cupped in the low-cut leotard bodice almost touch his head. Sometimes this quiets him completely. Most of the time he lets out a few cursory woofs then trots back into Khalida's studio where the rest of the group is waiting.

Every Thursday our ritual is the same. We are greeted by Solo and some human partner in the hallway. We hang up our coats in the closet, remove our footwear, and proceed to the kitchen where we help ourselves to herbal tea. Lemon mist, chamomile, Orange Zinger—we sip our tea and center our energies. Then we step into the studio to warm up.

The studio is a wide white room with a floor of honey-colored hardwood and a variety of unusual musical instruments hanging on the two smaller walls. Khalida has taught us their names: doumbec, def arqhool, rebaba. On one of the large walls is a mirror that spans the room. Across from the mirror, and approximately the same size, is a window through which we

Linda Watanabe McFerrin

can look down the hill toward the San Francisco Bay, where gray clouds of fog are usually creeping up toward us. Both views—mirror and bay—provoke the kind of shapeless reflection that makes me feel uncomfortable and a little bit sad.

Khalida is usually already in the studio, bells tinkling around her hips and ankles as she stretches toward the ceiling, folds at the middle, places her palms upon the floor. There is music playing on the boom box: classical Egyptian; Nubian music from Aswan; Arabic, Moroccan, or Turkish folk; baladi, malful, zaar, saaidi, and maqsoum rhythms—all sounds with which Khalida's acquainted us. The gentle thrum of the tabla baladi is relaxing.

I frequently arrive a little bit early so that I have time to surreptitiously watch Khalida exercise before she begins the class. I'm supposed to be warming up, too, but I can't keep my eyes off her. This is because Khalida and I are so different. I have shaggy dark hair, and I am a bit rotund. "Zaftig," as the Germans would say. Khalida has a more defined and close-to-perfect shape. She has curves, of course, like a great stretch of road or an elegant vase—curves that are flawless and comely. She wears low-slung skirts and a tight-sleeved choli that bares her white belly. Her belly is exquisite, rising from her hips like a small loaf of bread, warm and fresh from the oven. Her breasts are not large but fill the choli or the leotard and the Ghawazee vest that she sometimes wears to cup them. She has impeccable proportion and faultless balance. To understand this you would have to see Khalida move. She dances for herself, so her every gesture is self-contained, but she has a very definite relationship with the empty space around her. It's as if she were playing with it, teasing it into complicity, shaping it to her whims and purposes. Rooms move with Khalida. Open air caresses her. I don't really understand it, so I observe and admire.

Solo seems to share my obsession, but he is much more dogged in his adoration. He sits directly in front of Khalida, head in his paws, and stares at her, spellbound. Sometimes he makes little whining noises, and Khalida will stop for a moment and say, "Oh, Solo," and stroke his forehead and nose. This attention drives Solo to ecstasy. He bows his head, closes his chocolate-brown eyes, opens his mouth, and pushes back into her petting.

Khalida doesn't really share much of her life with any of us, but we can see it all around her. We see it in the photos of family that hang on her walls, in the pictures of dance competitions that she has won, in the portraits of old dance partners. I can't imagine what it must be like to make one's living by belly dancing. It seems extravagant, exotic, and daring. So Khalida is a puzzle to me. The modulation of her every word and movement is so carefully controlled that it seems to be choreographed. There's also her tranquillity, which is constant, and which I cannot figure out.

Of the six women in Khalida's class, no one knew anyone else when we started. None of us had taken belly dancing before, and that's a good thing because our mutual lack of coor-

Linda Watanabe McFerrin

dination is the only thing that keeps us together. That and our names. We have all adopted belly dancer's names. My name is Adilah. It means "one who deals justly." Ellspeth calls herself Basimah. This means "smiling one." Ellspeth-Basimah once said that she wanted to submit a videotape of our class to that TV show that features the funniest home videos. She was certain we'd win, and she was probably right, but we wouldn't let her bring her camera to class. Most of us weren't ready for that kind of national exposure.

In addition to Ellspeth-Basimah and me, there is Joan who's called Razi. Her name means "secret." Then there is Dierdre whose name, Faaria, means "pretty and tall." Sandy's belly dance name, Nafeesah, means "pure and refined," and Subba who is Middle Eastern just kept her own name. It means "eastern wind" or "zephyr."

From Khalida we are learning mostly the basics: posture, stretches, and strengthening exercises; slow, sensual movements like ribcage isolations, body waves, and belly rolls; as well as some fast, rhythmic steps. We can all see, of course, in the room's huge mirror, how ridiculous we look as we attempt to duplicate the movements that Khalida models for us, but Khalida is patient. She says each of us has a fascinating woman within. I don't see how she can be so patient. We have been taking her class for twelve weeks, since the latter part of last year, and we seem to have made little progress. In a another six weeks we are scheduled to give a recital. There is a big festival called Rakkasah that happens every year in Berkeley where many of the teachers showcase their workshops by having their students perform. The festival is outrageously popular. A pavilion is filled with booths selling everything from body jewelry to tattoos. There are piles of velvets, silks, combs, scarves, and spangles. It's just like an ancient bazaar. We will do two dances at Rakkasah. Ellspeth-Basimah says that we should strive for comedy since that's the effect we're going to produce, but most of us want to take ourselves and our abilities a bit more seriously. I have to admit that neither of our dances is looking serious yet. I am certain that we will horribly embarrass Khalida, but she doesn't seem to be worried at all. This is typical of the way she deals with things. We never know how she really feels.

I am trying to find my fascinating woman. My fascinating woman has gotten portly over the years. She has developed quite a set of hips and a belly that I have finally decided to put to use. I've made up my mind that I'm not going to run from my expanding girth anymore—I gave up jogging two years ago. Instead, I'm going to embrace it. I'm going to be proud of my ampleness. I think this is the direction I need to go, as I have not been successful in other ways. As a thin woman I found that I was a perfectionist. It seems to me that the heavier I get, the less controlling I become. As you can probably imagine, this is a huge relief.

Mainly I feel that in the past I have worried too much about what men think. Then why, you might ask, have I

Linda Watanabe McFerrin

taken up belly dancing? Well, I think I am doing it for myself, but I'm not sure it isn't just another way to try to find a guy. You know, it's an interesting coincidence, but since I started this class, I have found a new boyfriend. He is a professor at u.c. Berkeley, and I believe he likes me for my mind. I'm actually tired of people liking me for my mind. I'd really rather he liked me for my body. Thankfully, I started this class before I met him, so I can conclude that I am doing this for me, not him.

Khalida instructs us to warm up with a motion she calls "snake arms." This motion consists of sinuously undulating our upper appendages in sequence, first one, then the next, so that our arms resemble writhing serpents. Joan-Razi, who is standing right in front of me, is twisting her whole body along with her arms. She looks completely spasmodic, and it's difficult to refrain from comment. I am trying to keep my body straight as a rod as I provocatively wave my arms up and down. The effect is stiff and very robotic. I'm fairly certain that it's not provocative at all. It's all right. I'll get through it, like I get through most imaginative things—barely. I like math because if you put the numbers together right, there is no way you can get the wrong answer. I'm not proud of the fact that in just about everything else, I'm a klutz.

We progress to the next movement, which Khalida calls "maia." This exercise involves smoothly rotating our hips. I copy Khalida in an action that roughly simulates shifting from first to reverse with a sticky gear shift. This also feels terribly awkward.

I wonder if I will be able to smooth out this movement by the time we go to Rakkasah. I also have difficulties with shimmies, belly rolls, and ribcage isolations, but my worst problem is with the zils, or cymbals. We are supposed to clap away with our finger cymbals in a series of increasingly complicated rhythms that keep time to the music as our bodies perform the prescribed movements. Zil patterns include alternating right-left, standard right-left-right, military, baladi, and Moroccan Six. I simply cannot do any of it. I lose the beat almost immediately, and if I want to follow the steps at all, I have to settle for an occasional clink while everyone else's cymbals seem to be chattering rhythmically away. Khalida looks at me when I am hopelessly out of tempo and nods her head to the beat as if in doing so she can urge the right rhythms from me. This, of course, is not possible. I continue my convulsive clacking, and eventually she moves on to the next person, surprised, no doubt, that there exists one part of the universe that she cannot shape to her will.

I have decided that this doesn't matter. A few weeks ago our entire group went to a certain Moroccan restaurant where the belly dancing was reputed to be incredible. One of the principal dancers performed with a scimitar balanced on her head. I was entranced. I also noticed that every eye in the room was on that sword. My theory is that if I can balance a sword on my head, no one will pay much attention to the rest of me. It won't particularly matter what the rest of my body is doing. They'll

Linda Watanabe McFerrin

just think, *wow, look how she can dance with that sword on her head.* I can be a terrible belly dancer and still thrill the audience. And it wouldn't entail great feats of coordination. It would all be just a matter of balance. This is something I can do, so I commit to spending the next few weeks walking around with a book on my head. It's a shame that we won't be dancing with swords at Rakkasah. Then again, I might not be ready to graduate from a book to a scimitar, and I have a feeling that to do so prematurely could have grave consequences.

For our Rakkasah routines, there are no swords involved. Our first piece is performed to Egyptian rhythms. It is supposed to be a delectably sensuous dance. In the second piece we will use scarves. These are loads of fun. I suspect this number will bring down the house. Unfortunately, when we do our Egyptian swivel and dip across the room we look like an army of Frankenstein's monsters coming your way. Sandy-Nafeesah is actually the only member of the ensemble who is any good at this. The last to join our class, she is the most proficient in the group. She used to be a cocktail waitress, but now she is going to Berkeley, studying for a career in marketing. Maybe the cocktail waitressing helped her develop the grace. Joan-Razi, whose spastic gyrations I mentioned before, has stringy blonde hair and is very thin. It's odd that she's so thin because she's a caterer. I don't see how anyone around food all the time can be thin. Razi is the least graceful of all of us. I am not as gawky as she is. I am just short—short and chubby. Then there is

Dierdre-Faaria who is Amazon-tall. Dierdre's boyfriend is a musician, and she is taking Khalida's class to get his attention. I think it is working. Dierdre just found out a few weeks ago that she's pregnant. Khalida says dancing will be good for the baby, and we believe her. Actually, although we talk a lot about dance and movement, we talk very little about ourselves. Self-revelation is not in Khalida's repertoire. She doesn't like it when we chatter and gossip.

Khalida has won a lot of competitions. She has traveled all over the world as a dancer. She has studied almost every form of dance, including ballet and Butoh and ballroom dance, and she often incorporates the elements of those other forms into her choreography. She is famous for one movement that involves an arabesque that then winds into itself like a key turning into a lock. This and a certain Sufi-like whirl are her hallmarks.

When we dance, Solo is always among us. I don't know why Khalida lets Solo participate. I think he is incredibly spoiled, but I have to admit, he's also quite cute. Khalida's dog does everything with her. Sometimes, though, when she's really involved in her dancing, she ignores him completely. This leads me to surmise that dancing is definitely more important to Khalida than Solo.

When Khalida ignores Solo, he makes up to us. He sits in front of us when we dance. Sometimes he lies on his back and exposes his fat little belly. This means he wants someone to rub it. He's an outrageous flirt.

Linda Watanabe McFerrin

Two weeks prior to Rakkasah, Khalida has to go to a dance competition in Redding. She is taking Solo with her and has asked Farhannah to teach our Thursday night class so that we won't miss out on the practice. Farhannah is also a belly dancer. She and Khalida aren't exactly best friends, but they aren't rivals either. They are, however, radically different in style. Farhannah is a tall and athletic redhead who wears bright orange lipstick and a big Cheshire-Cat smile. Khalida is dark and sultry and usually grave. Farhannah loves to talk. Khalida keeps her own council.

At our very first class Khalida screened a video featuring various dancers illustrating different belly dancing methods and styles. Farhannah was one of the dancers. We all agreed that Farhannah has tremendous energy and a very acrobatic style. Basimah says disparagingly that she dances like a cheerleader, and I have to concur. Actually, Farhannah's dancing is very attractive. She wears tight vests and harem pants threaded with copper and gold. Coins bounce at her hips and her midriff. Her long legs and arms remind me of candles. She moves quickly when she dances, and with her red hair and orange lips and glittering coins, she looks just like she's on fire.

On that Thursday night, Farhannah doesn't show up until half past eight. We are all in the kitchen chatting away. The first words out of her mouth are, "Don't tell Khalida I was late. She'll be furious." Twelve heads swivel in unison to look at

Farhannah in a synchronization that, for us, is irreproducible. She certainly has our attention.

Razi is the first to spring to Khalida's defense. "Khalida never gets angry," Joan-Razi says.

"Oh, yes, she does," laughs Farhannah with a citrus-bright smile. "You just haven't seen it. Khalida has a terrible temper."

We look at one another in stark disbelief. Some of us want to know more.

"We don't believe you, Farhannah," Ellspeth-Basimah taunts.

"Well, believe what you want. I've seen it," Farhannah responds with great confidence, warming to her subject, quite pleased to knock Khalida off whatever pedestal she occupies in her followers' eyes. "By the way, does anyone want coffee?" she asks, taking a small bag of freshly ground beans from her purse. "I brought some hi-octane Pete's."

I want some. I'm tired of herbal tea, and I'm not the only one. We shift on our feet like nervous conspirators. A Benedict Arnold, I nod.

As Farhannah makes the coffee, we frame questions in our minds that will incite her to tell us more. This is easy. Farhannah squawks like a macaw at the least provocation. She's happy to spill the beans on Khalida's secrets.

"Khalida and I go back a long way," Farhannah reminisces, stirring then sipping her coffee. Her mouth leaves a big orange lip print on the cream-colored side of the mug. "We used to dance at the same cabaret. We weren't really friends," she confesses. "More like competitors at the time. We had such different styles." Farhannah smiles a flashy, bozo-bright smile at the thought of that ancient rivalry.

"Well, the first time I saw Khalida *really* mad was when she got angry at Michael." Farhannah's lips close over the side of the mug again. She just lets them rest there for a while, her green eyes screening some invisible movie. It looks like she isn't going to say anymore, and the story is just getting juicy.

"Who's Michael?" I query, just making sure that Farhannah's not going to drop the narrative ball.

"Oh, Michael was Khalida's boyfriend," says Farhannah, animated once more, happy to go on with her story. "Khalida always had bad luck with men. One boyfriend, Cholo, was her dance partner for years. That's when she was on the ballroom circuit. Cholo and Celia. Ostrich feathers and chiffon. Cha-chas and waltzes. Anyway, he was a real brute. He used to hit her and make really big bruises. Everyone tried to get Khalida to leave him, but she wouldn't. So, I guess it was partly her own fault. You know what they say, 'It takes two to tango.'" Farhannah pauses for a moment, very pleased with that expression. She sees that her audience isn't much interested in her cliché-spangled technique. We're dead set on the story.

"Anyway," she resumes, "that relationship went on for years until he left her for another dancer. He got a step-dancing Irish girl pregnant. She had several brothers—big Irish lads. I think Cholo met his match in that family.

"For Khalida, of course, it was the best thing that could happen, because after Cholo she met Michael." Farhannah stops at this point, takes a deep breath and looks around for her teaspoon. Razi sees it, grabs it, and hands it to Farhannah as fast as she can, in order to minimize interruption.

"So, what happened to Michael?" several of us prompt in another amazing example of unison.

"Well, to my knowledge, Michael is the only boyfriend Khalida has had who wasn't a dancer. Khalida was belly dancing, not partner dancing, when she met him. Michael was a photographer and quite an outrageous flirt. Most of us knew him. Khalida met him through a mutual friend. She needed promotional photos taken for an upcoming event, and Michael showed up to take them. Well, let me tell you, he fell head over heels for Khalida. The best pictures of her were taken by Michael. She has lots of them on the walls.

"The main problem with Michael, though," Farhannah continues, "was that he wouldn't stop flirting, and Khalida just couldn't stand it. She was furious with Michael most of the time, but the worst of it happened at a dance competition right here in Berkeley. Michael kept making up to a competitor from the east coast, a sloppy, raven-haired gypsy of a dancer, and Khalida was positively enraged. After that, Michael disappeared. Poof. Gone. Without even a trace. It was all so mysterious. The police questioned me. They questioned all of Michael's friends. They especially questioned Khalida, since someone told them about their big fight."

Farhannah's lips stretch merrily, at this point, into the shape of a long, carmine gondola. "They got zip. Niente. Nada. Zilch.

"I still don't know what really did happen to Michael," she muses as if in a trance. "If you want to know what he looks like, there's a photo of him on the wall, near the door. It's small. You may not have noticed."

We are all keyed up when we finally go into the studio that evening to work on our routines. Farhannah keeps us pretty entertained in our practice, as well. She can't believe how badly we dance. She corrects us constantly. She is much more hands-on than Khalida.

I'm determined not to have a good time. I already feel like a traitor. Before I leave I pause near the door to study the small photograph of Michael. There's no question, he's handsome. He has gentle, chocolate-brown eyes and dark, wavy hair. And he's smiling, flashing teeth that are strong, white, and sexy. Where have I seen that expression before?

When Khalida returns and we file into the kitchen the following Thursday, we are very subdued. Doubtless we're all flinching from the sting of our recent betrayals. It's as if we've allowed our teacher to be stripped of her costume. She dances before us, unwittingly naked, and we are all slightly embarrassed. Khalida senses, of course, that something is wrong. "You are all so quiet tonight," she observes. Solo also senses that something is wrong. He hangs next to her, behaving strangely protective. Our guilt makes us practice harder than ever.

The day of Rakkasah dawns much sooner than any of us seems prepared to accept, but we arrive at the auditorium early as Khalida has advised and find our way into the jungle of booths and stalls. Ellspeth-Basimah tells me that she is going to get a tattoo. Razi is trying on wigs. Later on, I find her stuffing herself with couscous and lamb shish-kebabs at the makeshift cafeteria. "You're going to have trouble dancing if you eat too much," I warn. Joan-Razi gives me a wry leer and surveys my dramatic dimensions. "I just don't think so," she says. It occurs to me that she is bulimic.

The day begins with special performances featuring professional dancers from around the world. Some are very large women. They shimmy and shake like walruses. Others are curvaceous and beautiful, a pleasure to watch as they undulate to the various rhythms. On the whole it's an uneven presentation, the worst, of course, being the students. We are worried that we'll be among the worst of the worst, but Khalida is unconcerned. She is talking with some of the other teachers. Farhannah is also there chattering away. We are all very nervous.

"You're going to be fine," Khalida assures.

I make a few really stupid moves, but overall, I'm happy with my performance. Somehow when I am whirling around on stage I lose my place and freeze like a rabbit in headlights. Just a hiccup. I rapidly find the rhythm again. Later while we are executing our Egyptian slide, I forget how to use my hips and begin to do something stiff and mechanical. Other than

Linda Watanabe McFerrin

this, I do rather well. I don't think we're marvelous. No miracle happens. We don't all of a sudden become fantastic belly dancers, but we are fine, just fine—obviously self-conscious, but nowhere near as bad as the Moroccan Mamas who are seven fat women making fun of their obesity. Once we leave the stage and a few more groups perform, I am jubilant.

It is, however, all a little too much for Bertrand, my Berkeley-professor boyfriend, who I've made the mistake of inviting and who really does love me only for my mind. I see it in his eyes at the end of the performance. Embarrassment. The basic and elemental fear of standing out in a crowd. Rakkasah takes hold of him like a migraine. Sick with overstimulation he makes his excuses and retreats to his syllabi.

I have no date for Khalida's party. It's a celebration of our successful recital and the culmination of the first phase of training. I'm pretty depressed about Bertrand's withdrawal. I end up drinking much more than I should, and giddy with wine, saying lots of things that I shouldn't. I ask Khalida about Michael. She is right in the middle of feeding Solo a biscuit. When she answers, Solo sits right down to listen even though Khalida has the biscuit still in her hand, still suspended in the airspace way over his head.

"Oh, he wasn't right for me," she says slowly.

It's amazing that she says anything because this is not the kind of information Khalida likes to share. That's all she says, then she turns her attention back to Solo and his biscuit. Solo's white teeth clap down hard, and he cracks away on it, his brown eyes never leaving Khalida's face.

"Who told you about Michael, anyway?" quizzes Khalida.

"Farhannah," I quickly and gladly confess. Then I tell Khalida everything Farhannah had said.

"Farhannah shouldn't have told you any of that," Khalida says frostily, and I get a glimpse of the anger that Farhannah told us about.

"Well, I don't think she meant any harm," I say in Farhannah's defense, toying with Solo's collar, realizing that I've gotten her into really big trouble. Solo looks regretfully up at me as if he knows exactly what a mess I'm making of things. I scratch his ear. He really does look familiar.

"She knows better," Khalida retorts. "This isn't the first time she's done this to me."

Khalida's party ends abruptly, after our talk. It seems I have put her in a hostile and crabby mood.

"Why did you say that to her, Adilah?" says Razi, shaking her head as she walks out the door.

"I'm lonely," I say weakly. "I've had too much wine. I'm sorry."

The last time I see Khalida is a week after Rakkasah. I go over to pick up some tapes she has ordered for me from a belly dance catalog—these should take me through a summer without her instruction. When I get to the steps I can hear Solo barking on the other side of the door. Khalida opens the door with her dog at her side. "Oh, hello," she says, without enthusiasm. "Come in.

Let's shut the door quickly. I don't want the cat to get out."

"You have a cat now?" I ask, somewhat surprised. I had thought for some reason that Khalida didn't like cats.

"Yes, I do," says Khalida, leaving me standing there as she goes to fetch the tapes.

Alone in the hall with Solo, I regard Khalida's dog. Solo lowers his head, eyes half closed, and thrusts his head under my hand, his big pink tongue lolling over the sexy white teeth. He's flirting with me, his look soulful, intense. I know where I've seen that face. I guess I suspected it for a long time. It doesn't bother me, though, probably because I know what it means to be lonely.

"Oh, Solo," I say, "I wish you were mine. I really need a dog like you. Wouldn't you like to come home with me? Come with me, Solo. When I open the door, you make a break for it."

Almost soundlessly Khalida steps back into the hall. "Here are the tapes," she announces harshly.

"Thanks, Khalida," I say, and I hand her my check.

Khalida opens the door. I head out, Solo following right behind me.

That's right, Solo, I say to myself. *Come with me. Be mine. Escape.*

Solo is standing on the peeling red steps with me when he turns to look back at Khalida.

"No, Solo," she says. "You come back here."

I gaze down to see Solo cast his warm, brown eyes up at me in a final farewell before turning and padding back to Khalida's side.

That's how I remember them. Khalida and Solo in the doorway, woman and dog, watching me to my car.

Behind them, Khalida's new, ginger-colored cat squawks out a meow that reminds me of a macaw and sharpens her claws on the rug.